THE BOY
WHO WAS
BURIED
THIS
MORNING

◆

VIKING
Mystery
Suspense

Other Dave Brandstetter Mysteries

Obedience

Early Graves

The Little Dog Laughed

Nightwork

Gravedigger

Skinflick

The Man Everybody Was Afraid Of

Troublemaker

Death Claims

Fadeout

Also by Joseph Hansen

Bohannon's Book (*stories*)

Steps Going Down

Brandstetter & Others (*stories*)

Pretty Dead Boy

Job's Year

Backtrack

A Smile in His Lifetime

The Dog & Other Stories

One Foot in the Boat (*verse*)

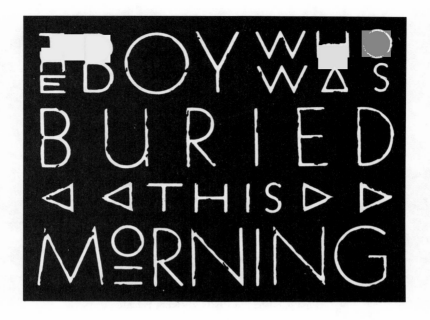

THE BOY WHO WAS BURIED THIS MORNING

JOSEPH HANSEN

A Dave Brandstetter Mystery

VIKING

C.2
M

VIKING
Published by the Penguin Group
Viking Penguin, a division of Penguin Books USA Inc.,
40 West 23rd Street, New York, New York 10010, U.S.A.
Penguin Books Ltd, 27 Wrights Lane, London W8 5TZ, England
Penguin Books Australia Ltd, Ringwood, Victoria, Australia
Penguin Books Canada Ltd, 2801 John Street,
Markham, Ontario, Canada L3R 1B4
Penguin Books (N.Z.) Ltd, 182–190 Wairau Road
Auckland 10, New Zealand

Penguin Books Ltd, Registered Offices:
Harmondsworth, Middlesex, England

First published in 1990 by Viking Penguin,
a division of Penguin Books USA Inc.

1 3 5 7 9 10 8 6 4 2

LIBRARY OF CONGRESS CATALOGING IN PUBLICATION DATA
Hansen, Joseph
The boy who was buried this morning / Joseph Hansen
p. cm.
ISBN 0–670–83324–X
I. Title.
PS3558.A513B69   1990
813′ .54—dc20   89-40648

Printed in the United States of America
Set in Times Roman

To Martin Fiddler Block
for a lifetime's cheerful friendship

THE BOY
WHO WAS
BURIED
THIS
MORNING

◆

1

◆

Fog made shapeshifters of the trees. It lay milky in the hollows and crept in tattered strands along the ridges. Brush crackled. Crouching figures in helmets and belted coveralls flitted through the fog, guns gave muffled pops, the figures dropped or dodged behind tree trunks. Voices clamored, far off. Someone yelped, "I'm hit."

"I didn't see any fog on the way here," Dave said.

"It ain't real," Roy Saddler said. "I bought the machinery off a movie studio that closed down." He hitched up his army fatigue pants. His heavy belly pushed them down again. He said proudly, "Only the Combat Zone gives you ground fog for your action pursuit games."

"Paintball," Enid Saddler said. She had a flat, prairie face, crinkled around the eyes, a flat, prairie voice. She wore a plaid cotton shirt and blue jeans. Her hips were skinny. She crossed her arms over flat breasts. "Paintball games," she told Dave. "That's what we'll be calling them from here on."

"Maybe you," Roy grunted. "Not me. Fancy-ass word. Shaves all the hair off it. Men don't play 'paintball.' " He sneered. "Men play action pursuit. Search and destroy. That's what men play." He coughed, hard, racked by the cough, bloated face turning red. He dropped his cigarette, stepped on it. " 'Paintball games.' " He wheezed. "Shit."

"It's not gonna get popular if folks think nobody comes but gun-crazy survivalists and soldiers of fortune and them," Enid said. "You heard that advertising man from the magazine—there's a real future for us if we can get people past the idea this is for roughnecks. It's healthy, wholesome outdoor recreation. Upscale, Roy—we got to go upscale."

"Sissified." Roy looked back toward the tall gateway framed of castoff telephone poles. Near this, among parked RVs, pickup trucks, and motorcycles, gangly, black-skinned Cecil Harris, beside a gleaming new Channel Three News van, held a microphone toward a bearded man with a beer can in his hand. Curly Ravitch, a balding youth in a droopy red sweat suit, trained a shoulder-mounted TV camera on the bearded man. Onlookers stood around, hip deep in fog. Roy said, "That killing done us more good than a million dollars worth of advertising in that asshole's magazine. After tonight's TV news and the morning papers, the Combat Zone will be the most famous outdoor recreation place in Southern California."

"If it don't close us down," Enid said.

"Don't talk crazy. Is it our fault a stray shot from some cockeyed deer hunter way up yonder in the hills hits one of our customers? Accident, like the cops said. Can't put us out of business. State's fault, not ours."

Enid opened her mouth to argue, but a young man came tramping out of the woods, looking dejected. "Got a cup of coffee for a dead man, Enid?" Pink fluorescent paint had splashed his military camouflage suit. For a moment, Dave mistook the gun that hung from his hand for an Uzi. It wasn't an Uzi. It was a toy. He pulled off a helmet that had a curved transparent face mask attached to it. Black makeup smeared his face.

Enid Saddler glanced at a watch on her bony wrist. "It's Licorice Luke, ain't it?" she said, and moved away toward a shacky building that was half catering counter, half supply store, beside which other young men and women in camouflage sat on fallen logs, drank out of cans or paper cups, ate, talked, laughed. "You didn't last long today. Sick or something?" She took his arm and they strolled together across lumpy, leaf-strewn ground toward the shack. Those already there looked up and jeered good-naturedly.

"Boy-howdy." Saddler chuckled and rubbed his hands together. "Build us barracks here, showers, mess hall, a real kitchen, serve real food. Be no stopping us after this."

Dave said, "The police report says nobody knew him."

"He was pretty new. He come regular, but always alone," Roy said. He gestured at the grubby group around the coffee shack. "You take most of these—they come three, four, five together. Teams. Know each other, know how to play the game together, tactics, strategy, which one is best at this, that, the other, quickest, smartest. But this here Vaughn, he never come with nobody. Just showed up, paid, bought paintballs if he had to, hung around till enough singletons come, or a team that needed another player. Wasn't long till they seen he was good, and he didn't have to wait." Roy pinched a short cigarette from a shirt pocket, lit it with a wooden match that he scratched on the seat of his pants, coughed. "Thing about him was—it wasn't a game to him." He cocked his head toward the laughing crowd. "Most of 'em that come don't take it all that serious." He looked into Dave's eyes with his bloodshot ones. "But this little Vaughn kid—he treated it like it was real combat, a matter of life and death."

Dave said, "That's how it turned out, didn't it?"

Roy shook his head, snorted. "Freak accident."

Dave pointed. Shaggy mountains loomed beyond the woods. "That's National Forest land, up there?"

"Full of fucking deer hunters," Roy said.

"Maybe you should close down for the season," Dave said.

Roy glared. "Don't go giving nobody else that idea."

Dave watched the foggy woods again, where the shadowy make-believe jungle fighters crouched and scurried, the funny guns popped, voices called near and far. "It's all lighthearted?" he said. "All in the spirit of fun?"

"Overgrown kids playing war," Roy said. He looked Dave up and down. "Cowboys and Indians in your time, right?"

"Cops and robbers," Dave said. "All my life."

Dave didn't really give a damn about this case—if it was a case. He was going through the motions because Cecil had asked him to. Cecil was worried about him. Dave was taking Max Romano's death too hard. Hell, Max was eighty when he died. The old restaurateur had had a long, cheerful run for his money, had certainly eaten and drunk his fill. Maybe it was surprising he'd lived so long. In the forty years Dave had known him, he'd always carried a lot of weight around. He'd only been thin once, a couple of years ago, when he'd tried to follow a diet on doctor's orders. He couldn't keep it up. It made him too miserable. Better to die fat and happy. Dave guessed Max had, if anybody ever did. At least it had been sudden. And in the surroundings Max loved best—his restaurant, laughing behind the bar.

But Dave hated his being dead, and hated what was about to happen to the restaurant. He couldn't tally how many meals he'd eaten at Max's down the years, how many friends he'd shared them with—some of those friends no longer living. Max had always kept a table for Dave in a far, quiet corner. Dave was having a lot of trouble picturing life without Max's. He'd be lost. The bright-eyed young nephew from New York had told him on a parched-grass cemetery hillside after the funeral that the restaurant's dark paneling, padded leather, stained glass were to be ripped out, in favor of white paint, beige carpeting, chrome-and-cane chairs, high walls of curved, clear glass. The rich foods and sauces were going too, to be replaced by the half-raw vegetables and pale, tasteless meats of nouvelle cuisine. The prospect made Dave shudder.

And this last week, in the hours when Cecil was away at the television station, Dave had slouched emptily around the house in the canyon, trying to read but staring blankly at the page instead, putting on tapes and when the music stopped not even noticing the silence, trying to watch old crime movies on the VCR and not seeing or hearing them. Forgetting to eat. Remembering to drink. Too often. Too much. Which was why Cecil had touted the strange death of Vaughn Thomas to him. To busy him with work. It was the best cure for grieving. Dave had learned that long ago. How Cecil knew it, young as he was, Dave couldn't say, but he was grateful to him, and now he was out here in the ugly world again, trying to pretend what he was doing mattered.

He rolled the quietly rumbling brown Jaguar along a tree-shaded street of dignified, well-kept old apartment buildings, looking for an address Cecil had given him. The place Vaughn Thomas had been living. Before that stray bullet had struck him down in the fake fog at the farthest reach of the Combat Zone. If stray bullet it had been. Cecil doubted it.

"He was keyed up," he told Dave. "Advertising is down at the end of the hall, but I pass there all the time. When his phone rang, he'd look at it like it was a rattlesnake. Sure, there were accounts out there, but there was something else out there too. And he didn't want to hear from it, whatever it was. Jumpy? You never saw jumpy till you saw Vaughn Thomas. Not running scared—sitting scared."

"You said he was a hater," Dave said.

Cecil nodded. "Niggers, Jews, Hispanics, Asians, you name it. Never to anybody's face. Too many of all those people around him all day long in the television business, the advertising business. But on the quiet, with that creep Kellaher in scheduling—you should hear the so-called jokes. 'How many blacks does it take to roof a house? Depends on how thin you slice 'em.' You know the kind."

"To my sorrow," Dave said. It was late at night. They sat on the long corduroy couch in the back building of the Horseshoe Canyon place. Shadows cast by a blaze in the big brick fireplace flickered in the rafters high above. They sat easy, legs stretched out. Dave sipped brandy, smoked, stared into the flames. "But haters make enemies."

"Just what I said. Vaughn Thomas dying by accident—I don't buy it. I don't care what Lieutenant Leppard says."

Dave sighed. "All right. I'll go with you tomorrow."

Now tomorrow was today. After wrapping up at the Combat Zone, Cecil had gone with his crew back to the studios in the hills near Dodger Stadium. Dave had come here to the quiet streets of West L.A. He found a parking place for the Jaguar and stepped along a sidewalk toward an archway into a patio with a mossy fountain, shrubs, ferns, an olive tree. He climbed red-tile steps to a white stucco balcony and rang a doorbell. Its sound suggested the apartment was empty. Maybe Jemmie—that was the only name Cecil could give him for the young woman Vaughn had been living with—maybe she was at the mortuary. He turned away, and went down the steps, where a short, stocky man was sweeping the patio. His hair was gray, his round face pink, pleasant, unlined as a baby's. He wore a faded Hawaiian shirt, ragged Bermuda shorts, sandals.

Dave showed him his license and said, "I'm looking for Jemmie."

"She is gone." He had a middle-European accent. "Yesterday, a well-dressed gentleman like you came by at noon, and not more than twenty minutes later, she departed. Suitcase in one hand, little Mike in the other. She had not even changed her clothes or combed her hair. In blue jeans, she left, and one of those bulky sweaters they like to wear. She had phoned for a taxi. It was out there waiting."

"Gone for good?" Dave said.

He blinked up at the apartment door. "She did not say." He gazed at Dave with brown eyes innocent as a child's. It crossed Dave's mind that eyes like that would be worth a lot to a liar. "She took her clothes, and little Mike's, but not Vaughn's. I went up to see. His clothes are still there. Maybe she will return for those." He grunted to himself, wagged his head. "Maybe not. He is dead, poor boy. Dead man's clothes, what use would she have for these?"

"She didn't speak to you when she left?" Dave said.

"Speak to me? She never thought of me." He lifted his arm to point with the broom handle and Dave glimpsed a blue tattoo, a concentration camp number. "That is my apartment over there. She could have stopped. I saw her—I see a lot from there. That window is like an extra television set." He went back to sweeping.

"She didn't tell you where she was going?"

"No, no. She did not even look my way." The broom whispered, the dry leaves whispered back. "I only learned later what it was about. On the TV news." He glanced briefly at Dave. "Young Vaughn got shot, killed. The well-dressed gentleman must have brought Jemmie the bad news."

"You'd never seen him before?" Dave said.

"I do not see everything. I have to sleep and eat."

"Did Jemmie look frightened?" Dave said.

The man made a neat pile of the leaves, then moved off to another quarter of the patio to clean up there. Dave followed. "She looked frightened most of the time."

"You seem an easy man to talk to, friendly," Dave said. "Did she ever tell you what she was frightened of?"

He leaned the broom against the rough gray rim of the fountain and held out his hand. "Kaminsky." He peered up with those soft, gentle eyes. "And you'd be . . . ?"

"Brandstetter. What frightened her, Mr. Kaminsky?"

"A man named Dallas, that is what I heard her call him." Kaminsky got the broom again and took up sweeping. "Big tall brute—long hair, looked like he came out of the—the wilderness, what you call the backwoods."

Dave put the folder away. "He came here?"

"Not long after Vaughn and Jemmie moved in."

"Had they come from the backwoods too?"

"I don't know where they came from, but they were in luck. It is not easy to find nice apartments in L.A. But the people who were going to take it never returned, so I had it empty and waiting the day Vaughn and the girl and her little boy showed up. He claimed they were husband and wife and Mike was his son—but it was a lie. Anyone could see that. Jemmie and Vaughn both had dark hair, dark eyes, delicate bones. You can tell even now—by the size of his hands—that Mike will grow up to be like Dallas, big and rangy. And blond—of course, that he is already."

"They weren't married," Dave said. "At least, on his job application at Channel Three he marked the 'single' box."

"Ja, well," Kaminsky said, "who cares about such details today?" He chuckled, marveling. "What importance we once attached to matters of no meaning."

"We still do," Dave said. "What did this Dallas want?"

"Jemmie. And Mike. Jemmie came to the door. For a moment, they just talked, then she began to shout at him. And he shouted right back at her. Both of them waving their arms. Very excited."

"Particulars?" Dave said.

"I could not hear." Now Kaminsky walked away. Out of sight, around a corner. In a minute he was back with a large green plastic bag and a square of cardboard. "One must be discreet." He knelt, pushed the sweepings onto the cardboard with the broom, and when Dave held the bag open for him, dumped them inside. With a small grunt, he rose and they repeated the process with the other three piles. "People are entitled to their privacy." He picked up the bulging bag, gathered the opening, and put a spin on it, then wired it shut with a quick twist of his fingers. "But what I saw I saw, and soon Vaughn came to the door. Dripping water. He had been in the shower, no? From down here, with that balcony in the way, he appeared naked. But when Dallas threw him down those stairs"—Kaminsky nodded—"I saw that he had wrapped a towel around his hips. I ran to my door and shouted I was calling the police. And nothing more was required. Dallas gave me one look, ran down the stairs, jumped straight over Vaughn, and was across this patio and gone."

"Was Vaughn hurt?" Dave said.

"Only his dignity." Kaminsky grinned. "But this was foolish, was it not? I mean, a man of six feet five inches versus one of five feet six? It was no disgrace. But he was disgusted with himself. 'Shall I call the police?' I said."

"Well, that made him stop swearing. He said, 'No thank you, Mr. Kaminsky. It was just a misunderstanding, among old friends.' "

"Was he afraid of the police?" Dave asked.

"The idea terrified him. That is what I think. I started to ask if Dallas was Jemmie's husband, Mike's real father." Kaminsky picked up the trash bag and started off with it. "But I have managed apartments long enough to know better than to pry."

"That's your guess, is it?" Dave called after him.

"That is my guess." Kaminsky once more disappeared around that corner. Dave waited. Then when he'd decided the interview was at an end, the man reappeared. "And it was not the last of this Dallas, either. He came back. Two or three times I saw him loitering in the neighborhood. Not an easy man to miss. The last time, Mike was out riding his plastic tricycle up and down the sidewalk, and I happened to glance out my front window, and here was Dallas, squatting down, talking to the child. I wasted no time. Immediately I went out there. And as soon as he saw me, he left. He had an old pickup truck with a camper on it. Got in this and rattled off. He did not return again. Not that I know of."

"Did you tell Jemmie about it?"

"Of course, right away. She was in the laundry room. Turned white as the sheet she was folding, and ran out and fetched Mike and his wheels, and after that she never let him outdoors again, not unless she was with him."

"Was her last name Dallas?" Dave asked.

Kaminsky shook his head. "She referred always to herself as Mrs. Thomas, Mrs. Vaughn Thomas. She seemed proud of it." Kaminsky glanced up at the closed door of the Thomas place. "A country girl, you know? Curious match. Vaughn wasn't like this at all. College boy, rich boy. Spoiled. Sulky much of the time." Kaminsky snorted. "He did not like me. He did not like my name. Always he sneered it, smirking. 'Ka-*min*-sky.' What do people like that think—that only people named Thomas have a right to be here?"

"People like that don't think." Dave looked toward the archway and the street beyond. "A country girl. But you never asked her where she came from? She never told you?"

Kaminsky scratched his forehead, thinking. "Horses," he said at last. "She grew up around horses. That much she did say. And I believed her." He gave a nod to himself and told Dave, "Girls crazy about horses are different, not just here in America, but all over the world. Did you ever notice that? A little bit—what shall I say—boyish?"

"Dallas will know where she came from. He came from the same place." Dave turned away, turned back. "You didn't happen to get his license number, did you?"

Kaminsky looked abashed. "I am sorry."

"Don't feel bad." Dave moved off. "I'll find him."

"Wait." Kaminsky hurried after him. "It had a bumper sticker. Shocking. A double lightning bolt, faded, peeling. Like the Waffen SS." He stopped in front of Dave. "The TV news called Vaughn's death an accident." Plainly excited about being part of a murder investigation, he was also worried, anxious. "You think Dallas killed him?"

"I think it would be easy to walk into the Combat Zone carrying a real gun," Dave said. "No one would notice."

2

◆

Ngawi Smith unfolded from his yellow cab in hinged lengths of
white-clad leg that when he was fully upright had him towering over
Dave. "No, sah," he said happily, showing rows of terrific white
teeth. He pushed an embroidered African cap back on his neatly
barbered head. "I remember her because she was so frightened. She
held on to the little boy in the back seat here"—he gestured with a
long-fingered hand, as if Jemmie and Mike were still his
passengers—"as if someone wanted to snatch him from her, and she
kept looking out the rear window every few seconds, afraid we were
being followed. 'No one is following us,' I told her. I would know,
you see." He bent his knees slightly, and for a moment used a
shirttail to polish the mirror fastened to the door. "I always know
when that is happening."

"Does it happen often?" Dave said. The sun glared off the pale
yellow stucco of the Greyhound bus station at the beach and made
him squint. *Placa* had been spray-painted on the stucco, in black, in
red, as high as human arms could reach—messages, boasts, threats,
in symbols and codes only gang members could read. There had been
less of this the last time Dave had passed here. There was so much of
it now, it was all tangled up. He expected it would soon be painted
over. Again. "Are you followed a lot?"

"When I am," the tall black said, "I find a well-lighted place, a shopping mall parking lot maybe, and swing in there, and stop the cab, and get out, and open the door for the passenger, and order him out. I am not getting assassinated for the sake of a cab fare. There is a lot of shooting going on in the streets these days. And with these AK-47s and the other automatic rifles, everyone dies. Not just the target. They cannot really be controlled."

"You get a nice class of passenger," Dave said.

Smith raised and lowered his shoulders. "They look like anyone else. But their bags do not contain clothing. Drugs perhaps? Bundles of cash? Videotape masters? Who can say? They are almost always on their way to the airport. But if they wish to risk their lives in crime, that is no affair of mine. I dare not be killed or even wounded. I have a family in Nigeria, and it is my plan to save enough money to bring them here. My mother, my wife, my two children."

"A hell of a place to bring anybody," Dave said.

"Ah." Smith grinned. "You do not know Nigeria. Now, Nigeria—that is a 'hell of a place.'" He laughed.

Dave sighed, turned, looked across the street to the palisades, lawns, flower beds, old palm trees, railed paths, the ocean a gunmetal color with the sun glaring off it. Fancy kites bobbed and swooped above the beach, trailing ribbons. Gulls soared and cried. "Jemmie Thomas had one suitcase, is that right?"

"Rather a large one, and heavy." Smith nodded. "As if it contained all her worldly goods. Brown simulated leather. Soft. And a handbag, one of those large, shapeless ones, worn over the shoulder on a long strap."

"And you don't know where she was headed?"

"I carried the grip for her into the station, and set it at the ticket counter," Smith said. "She put a dollar in my hand and thanked me. A dozen persons were lined up to buy tickets. I could see out the window, someone had already got into my cab here at the curb. So I did not stay long enough to learn to what destination she bought a fare. Sorry." He frowned, and bent above Dave, craning a long neck. His breath smelled of chewing gum, sweet, spicy. "Can you tell me? What was she so frightened of?"

"Somebody shot the man she was living with," Dave said. "Not in her presence. He was away, playing weekend games. Action combat. You ever hear of it?"

Smith looked blank and shook his head.

"It's like military exercises," Dave said, "only just for fun. They pretend to be soldiers, dress up in camouflage outfits and run around in the woods, potting at each other with balls of paint."

Smith laughed disbelief. "What a mad country. Do they not know that war is not a game? Where I come from—"

"Not most of them," Dave said. "Too young."

"And someone killed him there?" Smith said.

"He knows it wasn't a game," Dave said. "Now."

"And his wife—Jemmie. She too knows." Smith drew in air sharply. "Does she know who did it?"

"Looks that way," Dave said, "doesn't it?"

"She was young." Smith took off his beautiful cap and turned it in his fingers, watching it thoughtfully. "She would have living parents. Perhaps she was only running home." That his own home was hopelessly far away hollowed his voice. "That is what we all wish to do at such times."

"The wish doesn't stop, even when there's no home to go to." Dave watched a blue-and-white bus spattered with dried mud creak up off the street and pass in, roaring, at the smoky entryway of the station garage. "I have to find out where Jemmie Thomas's home is. And I haven't much time. Thanks." He poked a ten-dollar bill into the shirt pocket where Smith kept a fasces of ballpoint pens. Smith put his cap back on. Dave crossed sandy sidewalk to the hand-smeared glass double doors of the station and pushed inside.

Passengers from the newly come bus trailed with their luggage into the waiting room. The blue-and-white paint of the room was scratched, scarred, incised with initials, sprayed with graffiti. Coin-operated television sets bolted to chrome plastic-cushioned chairs had gray faces. All but one. A pair of brown-skinned little kids in Levis and King Kong T-shirts watched cartoons on that one. They occupied the same chair and wiggled, elbowed, and kicked each other without once taking their glossy brown eyes from the muscular warriors snarling and shooting fire-spitting assault rifles on the tube. Field workers with straw hats pulled down over their eyes slept on other chairs. Women guarded scuffed suitcases and twine-tied cartons. A stubbly-haired blond teenage boy in grubby yellow surfer trunks leaned beside a door whose sign said MEN. He looked bored, but he was watchful. He noticed everybody who came and went. When his look caught Dave's, he smiled sourly, and his dull blue eyes said, *Do you want me? You can have me*.

Dave got into line at the ticket counter where one station was open, three closed. It seemed longer, but in five minutes he was facing a fat black agent who wore a blue uniform with a jauntily tilted cap. Dark glasses covered her eyes, but he sensed her totting up the cost of his clothes, sensed her wonder at meeting here a man who had that kind of money. But she merely smiled a practiced smile and asked him where he wanted to go.

He showed her his license and said, "Yesterday, at two in the afternoon, a small, dark young woman with a little blond boy about five or six years old took a bus out of here. Blue jeans and a sweater, one suitcase and a shoulder bag. Do you remember her?"

"I'm afraid I don't," the agent said. "I'm sorry, but I see too many people. 'Less they dressed in a gorilla suit or something, I'm not likely to remember."

"I need to know where she went," Dave said. "It could be a matter of life and death."

The woman flipped open a loose-leaf book. "Yesterday, at two?" She ran a finger down a plastic-covered printed list. "Buses that next hour left up the coast for Santa Barbara, inland for Santa Ana, and down south for San Diego"—she looked up—"so that don't exactly narrow it down for you, does it? I'm sorry."

"Thanks for trying," Dave said. He turned to leave the counter and felt a bump. "Excuse me," he told the little old woman behind him. Her face was brown and deeply wrinkled by sun, weather, years, and when she opened her mouth to speak he saw she had no teeth. She said in Spanish:

"The little sparrow has taken your wallet."

Dave turned in time to see a flash of yellow disappear into the garage. He ran that way. The garage was a bleak cement cavern that smelled of exhaust fumes, gasoline, tires, and five hundred thousand miles of country highway. Greasy-handed men in coveralls serviced engines. Filipino women with hair wrapped in white vacuumed inside the buses, sprayed and wiped windows. Drivers leaned against the buses, smoking, laughing, tilting up shiny cans of soda pop.

Dave stepped quickly among the buses, looking this way, that way, but the little sparrow had flown. Dave tried a door at the rear of the garage and found himself in a gritty, sunstruck lane parked tight with cars of citizens playing truant on the sand. Far down the lane, a boy and a girl lifted purple surfboards out of the back of a pickup truck. A fifty-year-old skate-boarder with skin like leather and white hair on his sagging chest zigzagged between the parked cars. But yellow tail had vanished.

Wanly, Dave slid a hand into the inner jacket pocket where he'd kept his wallet. The touch he'd felt there had been light and fleeting. Funny. He'd marked the kid for a hustler. Instead he was a pickpocket, and a good one. With a wry laugh and a shake of his head, Dave started along the lane, peering into trash modules. Sometimes they took only the cash and threw the rest away.

On the red-tile doorstep of the large, white Spanish colonial that rose back of trees on a long, broad slope of lawn and flower beds in Beverly Hills, he waited for such a time that he began to wonder if anyone was home. Then the carved door with its black wrought-iron knocker opened, and a young man looked at him. He was in shirt sleeves, the knot of his necktie dragged down, bluish beard stubble on his smooth jaws. He wore his hair long, like a rock musician. But it needed tending to. He looked frazzled, exhausted. A blue pencil was between his teeth. He took off horn-rimmed glasses and blinked at Dave with eyelashes so dense, black, and long they looked artificial. His eyes were bloodshot.

"Yes?" he said. "What is it?"

"Dave Brandstetter"—he held out a business card—"to see Mr. and Mrs. Thomas, please?"

"Mr. and Mrs. Thomas just lost their son," the young man said. "They're tired of being pestered. They deserve some privacy, for Christ sake."

"I won't stay. I'm a private investigator, looking into the disappearance of the young woman Vaughn was living with."

The young man jerked in surprise. "Disappearance?"

"I thought the Thomases might know where she's gone." Dave stepped at him, and he reflexively backed off. In the cool entryway, Dave took the door from him and closed it. "I know it's an intrusion, but it's important."

"They don't know anything about her," the young man said. "They only met her once."

Dave said, "Who are you? What do you know about her?"

"O'Neil." The young man pushed the glasses into a shirt pocket and held out his hand. "Neil O'Neil. I work for Thomas Marketing. I'm Mrs. Thomas's assistant."

Dave shook his hand and let it go. "And Jemmie? Did you ever meet her?"

O'Neil turned his head, looked at Dave from the corners of his eyes. "Private investigator? Working for whom?"

"Channel Three." It was as good a lie as any. "Their employee insurance company. Perhaps she went home. Do you know where that is?"

O'Neil shrugged. "Some backwoods place. All she had to do was open her mouth for you to know that. Her daddy breeds saddle horses. That's all I know."

"A place with no name?" Dave said.

"Not that I ever heard. You see, Vaughn went—"

From some place far off and high up in the house a woman's voice called, "Neil—where the hell are you? Who is the fascinating conversationalist—Dr. Samuel fucking Johnson?"

"Jesus," O'Neil said. He turned and started toward a tiled, iron-railed, spiral staircase housed in a white-walled round tower with slit windows. "You'll find Mr. Thomas in there." He gestured at an archway and ran up the stairs two at a time.

Dave called after him, "Ask Mrs. Thomas to come down for a moment, please?" Dave waited at the stair foot. Faint sounds leaked down to him, the beeping of electronics, the whine of a computer printer, the electronic ring of a telephone. Was this a house in mourning? It sounded more like business as usual.

"I'm really terribly busy." A woman in her mid-forties came down the stairs with a clack of heels. She was dressed in blousy clothes, scarves, pants—the dominant color was peach. Even her hair was peach. "Just what is it you want to know?"

"Jemmie's whereabouts," Dave said.

She yelped a mirthless laugh. "Jemmie. What in the world makes you think I know Jemmie's whereabouts? Or care?"

"She meant a lot to your son," Dave said.

"She was nothing but redneck trash. I can't think how a boy with Vaughn's upbringing, with all his advantages, could choose a girl like that. A married woman. And with a child. Vaughn was only a child himself." Sylvia Thomas had stopped halfway down the stairs. Now she turned and started up again. And stopped. And looked down at Dave once more. "I don't believe for a minute she 'meant a lot to my son.' I believe he only took up with her to spite me."

"Sylvia!" In the archway O'Neil had pointed out to Dave an old man stood, a drink in his hand. Steven Thomas looked like Dave, reedy, six feet tall, blue eyed, with a thick shock of expensively cut white hair. But he was ten years older, with a river map of tiny broken red veins across nose and cheekbones. "Control your mouth. You always hated him. Always. Always correcting him. Always finding fault. To your mind he never did anything right. And then when he brought Jemmie and little Mike here, you turned them away."

"She had a husband," Sylvia said. "What kind of mother would allow her son to cohabit with a woman like that under her own roof? You were always a fool about Vaughn. Anything he wanted he got. You spoiled him rotten. And every time he was in trouble, you made excuses for him, you bought his way out. If you'd used a little discipline on him, he'd have respected you, he wouldn't have run wild."

"Will you shut up?" the old man shouted, red in the face. "He's dead. And it's your fault, your fault, Sylvia. If he'd been living here where I could have looked out for him . . . but no. Oh, no. When we thought he was dead—when we thought we'd never see him again—and he came back, did you welcome him with open arms? No. You drove him away. The language you used on that poor little girl of his—"

"She was a tramp and a troublemaker," Sylvia said. "Steve, I really haven't time for this. I've got a thousand loose ends to clear up on the Sweepstakes." She climbed the stairs. "Talk to the nice man. Tell him your troubles."

Dave called, "Where did Jemmie come from, Mrs. Thomas? Where did Vaughn find her?"

"I don't know, but wherever it was"—Sylvia Thomas reached the top of the stairs, and moved out of sight, heels clicking—"he should never have gone there." A door slammed.

Mutely, Steven Thomas led Dave down short stairs into an immense living room furnished by a decorator who might not have wished to remain invisible but surely had managed it. Everything here was costly and well made but none of it had any distinction. Thomas went to a bar at the room's end.

"What do you want?" he said.

"Jemmie has disappeared," Dave said. "I have to find her. It's an insurance matter."

"Disappeared?" Thomas set a whiskey bottle down, frowning. "When? I talked to her yesterday, at noon." He winced. "She loved Vaughn. And the police came here to notify us, but they didn't know about her. She and Vaughn weren't married, you know. I mean, she only just filed for divorce a few weeks ago, so it had to be me, didn't it? To tell her about—about Vaughn—what happened to him."

"Divorce from whom? What was her married name?"

Thomas frowned. "By God, I don't think I ever heard."

"Dallas? Does that ring a bell?"

A head shake. "Sorry. You say she's run off?"

"She left right after you did. Where would she go?"

"I don't know." Thomas took a quick swallow from his glass, then looked at Dave. "A drink, Mr. Brandstetter?"

"Scotch, thank you." Dave walked with him back to the bar. The label on the bottle Thomas chose read Laphroaig. Dave had never run across it before, but he'd heard of it. The neck of the bottle rattled against the glass.

Dave said, "Vaughn's mother didn't go with you?"

"Vaughn's mother"—Thomas handed Dave his glass—"is long dead. Sylvia is—was—his stepmother." He glanced toward the hallway. "Please excuse the scene—we're both upset. You understand. She loved Vaughn as if he were her own son." Thomas drank deeply of his sour mash. "But she's just winding up the biggest marketing campaign in our shop's history." He peered at Dave, almost pleadingly. "You've heard of it, of course—the Shopwise Supermarket Sweepstakes? You've seen the promotion on television?"

Dave watched only CNN and videotapes. But he nodded.

"There's no way to stop these things or even take a breather, once they're underway." Thomas went and dropped into a white easy chair, part of a group near an arch-shaped fireplace. He waved at another chair, and Dave took it. "Truth is," Thomas said, "Sylvia runs Thomas Marketing these days." He twitched his mouth, disgusted, resigned. "I'm past it. Angina. Can't even climb stairs anymore."

"I think the girl went home." Dave tasted the Scotch. Glorious. "Where would that be, Mr. Thomas?"

The old man shook his head. "Vaughn disappeared, you know, last winter. And—" He waved a hand. "No, let me start at the beginning, so you'll understand. He got booted out of college. Most unfair thing that ever happened. Cleared his name, you know, but he was hurt. He wouldn't go back. Tried working for Thomas Marketing, but he was restless. Lasted two years, but it was an awful strain on him. Loved the outdoors. Action. Nervous boy. Couldn't stand being cooped up, trapped behind a desk. Had these dreams of being a soldier of fortune." With a mournful smile, Thomas took a swallow from his glass. His hands trembled, jingling the ice. "And on his twenty-first birthday, he went to the lawyers and collected a little money his mother had left him, and took off." Thomas gestured in the air. "Not a word to me or Sylvia, not a word at the shop. Just vanished. Then just as suddenly, three, four months later, he was back. From where, he never said. Might have—but Sylvia wouldn't have him here at home where we could talk. He worked for her at Thomas Marketing for a little while, then quit again and went to work at the television station. I hardly saw him. He never even tried to talk to me." A tear ran down Thomas's face. Bleakly, he brushed it away.

"How far would his mother's money take him?"

Thomas moved his shoulders. "Five thousand dollars?"

"What kind of trouble?" Dave said. Thomas's white brows went up in confusion.

"You said he got into trouble in college."

"They claimed he painted swastikas on a Jewish fraternity house," Thomas said scornfully. "No truth in it, of course. Ridiculous. He was unlucky enough to be in the vicinity when the campus police patrol car answered the call. He was running. He'd seen the mischief. He didn't want any part of it. Course not." Thomas knocked back the rest of his whiskey. "Good Lord. He was raised among advertising people, television people. Half the guests in this house down the years have been Jewish. Sylvia is Jewish, for heaven sake. How could he be anti-Semitic? But he had the red paint on his hands. And they were going to get him because they couldn't find the ones who really did it. Well"—Thomas's mouth twisted in a wry smile over expensive false teeth—"my lawyers were too much for them." He sighed. "But . . . that ended college for Vaughn." Thomas pushed up out of his chair. "Seemed to him like the world was against him." Thomas wandered back toward the bar. "He was getting into one scrape or another from the time his mother died." Thomas clinked ice into his glass. "I was too busy building the business. Never took time off to be a father to him." He filled the glass and left the bottle open. "So much older too. When I married

Sylvia, I hoped things would be better. Young, you know. She did her best, at least by her own lights, but it was too late."

"Who would have wanted to kill him?" Dave said.

"What?" Thomas's glass tilted. Whiskey spattered his trousers. He stared at Dave, appalled. "Kill him? It was an accident. The police said so. A deer hunter—"

Dave set down his glass and rose. "If it was an accident, why did Jemmie take Mike and run? She loved Vaughn. Why didn't she stay to see him buried?"

Thomas seemed to wither in his chair. He nodded bleakly. "She was afraid. I could see it in her eyes, as soon as I told her he'd been killed. I knew the look. Vaughn had it too when he came back from wherever he'd been those months. He was suntanned, trim, healthy. It was plain he'd had a good jolt of what he liked best—God's great outdoors. But you could see in his eyes he was afraid, Mr. Brandstetter. Deathly afraid."

"It looks like he had reason, doesn't it?" Dave said.

Thomas's voice trembled on the edge of tears. "I wanted to believe it was an accident," he said.

3

◆

Detective Sergeant Joey Samuels was a pale man, skin, hair, eyes—always had been. Two years ago, trying to save Dave's life, on a rainy day on a steep Hollywood side street, he'd taken a bullet in his chest. It had come close to killing him, kept him hospitalized for months and an invalid at home for a long time after that.

That Samuels should trail Dave on a case to prevent his being harmed had been Captain Ken Barker's idea—not Dave's. So it wasn't rational for Dave to blame himself when the crazy kid he was pursuing had shot Samuels—it wasn't rational, but he'd blamed himself all the same. He'd gone often to the hospital to see Samuels. He'd visited him at home, taking him books, records, elegant foods, flowers for Sophie, his wife, toys for his small son, Pepper.

But this was the first time he'd run into Samuels at his green metal desk in the wide green detective's room at the Glass House—LAPD headquarters downtown. The place was noisy with telephones, typewriters, clicking computer keyboards, whining printers, slamming file drawers, and the loud voices of police officers. And that Samuels looked as if he'd never had a day's pain made Dave feel better. Samuels smiled, stood up, shook Dave's hand, sat down.

"Lieutenant Leppard had to go out. He left the file with me." He laid a pale, thick hand on the thin folder in front of him. Around it lay stacks of files, loose forms, photographs. It was a busy desk. They were all busy. Los Angeles had more murders in a month than most countries in the Western world tallied up in a year. Weekends were nightmares now—eight to a dozen drive-by gang shootings from Friday night to the dawn of Monday morning. And it was getting worse. "The bullet blew half his head away," Samuels said, "but there's no way except accident that bullet will ever be found in those woods. So we don't know what kind of gun it was—high-powered, large-caliber, that's it."

"Did you know he was living in West L.A. with a young woman called Jemmie, and her five-, six-year-old boy?"

Samuels opened the folder, bent and blinked at it. "The address in his wallet was in Beverly Hills. His father and mother's house."

"Stepmother," Dave said. "Sylvia—she runs Thomas Marketing. The old man wanted him there, but Sylvia took against the girl, so Vaughn went off with her to live on his own—though he worked for Sylvia for a while."

"Yeah—we got that part. Then he went to work for Channel Three, selling advertising." Samuels smiled a pale smile. "That Sylvia, she's a dynamo," Samuels said. "But she didn't say anything about the girl. Or about her son—stepson—not living at home." He tilted his head. "You don't expect lies when you go to tell parents their son has been shot to death. Do you?"

"You expect lies wherever you go," Dave said. "In this case, I wouldn't attach much importance to it. She hated the girl, was furious and ashamed at the boy she'd raised taking up with what she called a redneck. She wouldn't want strangers to know, especially not official strangers, and she wouldn't want it in a police report, where it could be picked up by the six o'clock news."

Samuels laughed wryly and shook his head.

"But you have to look at that apartment." Dave gave him the address. "There might be a lead there. Jemmie ran away for a reason. Vaughn's father went and told her the bad news right after you'd told him. He said it terrified her. The manager said she was out of there in twenty minutes, running scared. The taxi driver told me she kept looking back, afraid someone was following her to the bus station."

Samuels frowned, tilted his head. "She figured the one who killed her boyfriend was going to kill her too?"

"And she was probably right," Dave said.

"Why—what the hell had they done?" Samuels said.

"Did his folks tell you," Dave asked, "that on his twenty-first birthday, Vaughn collected five thousand dollars from his late mother's estate and took off for points unknown and stayed away for three or four months?"

"Yeah, I guess somebody mentioned it," Samuels said.

Dave nodded at the file. "Look in there, and see if they by any chance dropped a place name. They told me Vaughn wouldn't tell them where he'd been."

Samuels made to turn over a page in the folder, then closed it instead. "I don't have to look. I remember. They said he wouldn't talk about it."

"He brought the girl and the little boy back with him from wherever it was," Dave said. "Steven Thomas said Vaughn looked like he'd spent those months outdoors. Kaminsky called Jemmie a country girl. O'Neil, Mrs. Thomas's assistant, told me her father breeds horses."

Samuels sighed. "We could check lists of horse breeders, if we knew her name. Jemmie what?"

"Her father's name wouldn't help. She was married—probably to a big, rangy, long-haired ranch-hand type who came and raised hell at the apartment one day. Kaminsky heard Jemmie call him Dallas. But it could be a first name. Anyway, Jemmie never called herself Dallas. Always Mrs. Thomas. Even before she filed for divorce."

"I wish people wouldn't keep secrets," Samuels said.

"I've got to find her." Dave read his watch and rose. "Before Vaughn's killer can find her and kill her too."

"We'll search the apartment." Samuels reached for his telephone. "I'll let you know if we find anything."

◆

Dave ran out of energy with unexpected suddenness these days. When the Jaguar, scraping its underside, lurched down off crooked, slanting Horseshoe Canyon Trail into the brick forecourt of his house, he was tired. He parked the car as always beside the row of French doors that made the front wall of the front building of this oddly laid-out place, turned off the engine, and sat for a minute dully, trying to think of something to like about growing old. He couldn't think of anything.

With a sigh, and a little stiffly, he climbed out of the car, closed the door, and locked it, the motions mechanical. The brush and scrub oak that edged the brick paving needed trimming again. He liked them overgrown, but there was, he supposed, a limit. Stumbling a little on the uneven bricks, he walked around the shingled end of the front building. Fallen leaves from the oak that spread gnarled limbs to shade the main courtyard crackled under his soles. He hadn't eaten lunch, so he veered toward the cookshack, its low roof sheltered by tall eucalyptus—then changed his mind. He lacked what it took even to decide what to eat, let alone to fix it.

In the back building—it had once been a stable and it still, in rainy weather, smelled faintly of horses—he trudged over beautiful Navajo rugs, past the couch that faced the big, raised hearth fireplace of distressed brick, past his desk and computer and files, to the bar, where he took an icy glass from the little refrigerator and built a double martini for himself. Maybe it would revive him. Maybe it would make him hungry. Then he wearily rummaged records from the files, sat at the desk, put on his reading glasses, and began phoning about his stolen credit cards. It took half an hour. The martini stunned him. He had what it took only to unplug the phone, climb the raw pine stairs to the sleeping loft, rid himself of jacket, trousers, shoes, socks, tie, and fall, already half asleep, onto the bed. He'd had a glimpse of blue through the skylight then.

When the hammering of the door knocker below woke him, the sky was streaked with red. He tried to call out, but only a rasp came. Blinking, struggling to get upright and swing his feet to the floor, he cleared his throat and shouted, "Just a minute, please. I'm coming." His shirt was rumpled and sweat-soaked. He peeled it off, found a clean sweatshirt in a drawer, pulled this on, kicked into sweat pants. In the mirror over the unpainted pine chest of drawers, he saw his hair was rumpled. He couldn't locate a comb. To hell with it. He thumped barefoot down the stairs.

He blinked at the young man with attaché case standing outside the door in the sunset glow. "O'Neil?" he said.

"Sorry to bother you." The olive-skinned youth eyed Dave worriedly. "Are you okay?"

"I was just having myself a nap," Dave said. "Come in. It's all right." He backed up, gestured at the room. O'Neil came in, a little hesitantly, and Dave let the door stand open. The air outside seemed cooler than in here. That was the effect of the sun striking the glass of the skylights in warm weather. "I sleep too much. Sit down." He pointed to one of two red leather wing chairs flanking the fireplace. Bookshelves loomed to the rafters beside them. "It's quite a drive up here. Like a drink?"

"That's very kind." O'Neil set his attaché case by the door and went to sit in the wing chair. "I don't drink. Have you got a soda?"

Dave went back to the bar. O'Neil called, "I live in Burbank, so this place is really on my way home. And I wanted to explain some things to you. You must have gotten a pretty bad impression of Syl—of Mrs. Thomas today."

Dave laughed. "I hardly had time."

"This Shopwise campaign is terribly important to her," O'Neil said. "It's been terrifically successful, but it's been a lot of work. Thomas Marketing will be among the top ten in the country now. But it's almost killed her." Dave handed him a tall glass of ice cubes and a cold can of Coke. The young man smiled. "And me too. All of us. Talk about tension. Talk about stress." He looked at the can and glass in his hands. "Thank you."

"You're welcome." Dave sat on the couch. He'd brought orange juice for himself. Plain. No booze. It tasted good.

"Vaughn quit because of the pressure," O'Neil said. "He hated that campaign. That's why he went to work at Channel Three."

"Was that it?" Dave said.

"Yes, that was it." O'Neil's hand shook, pouring the drink. He glanced at Dave sharply as he set down the red-and-white can. "Did Steve tell you it was something else?"

"We didn't talk about it," Dave said. "Steve did say Vaughn didn't like desk work. He liked the outdoors. You told me Jemmie's father breeds horses. What else do you know about her?"

O'Neil studied Dave puzzledly for a few seconds. "Why is she important? I only met her once or twice, and we never really talked much, but she didn't strike me as very bright. A really nothing girl. I don't know what he saw in her."

"She's important because she ran away," Dave said. "It wasn't for nothing. Either she knows who killed Vaughn and figures that person knows she knows. Or she knows the reason Vaughn was killed, and thinks the killer will guess that and come after her. Or both. What did Vaughn tell you about her? Anything—I don't care how trivial."

O'Neil seemed dazed for a second, then shrugged. "Only that he was crazy about her. She was the sweetest, prettiest, most honest girl he'd ever met. But he and I hardly ever saw each other except at the store, and when I'm at the store, I'm pretty much always with Sylvia. And he wouldn't mention Jemmie where Sylvia could hear and make a comment."

"All right," Dave said. "He didn't ever happen to mention Jemmie's last name? Her father's name? Her husband's? She was married, you know."

Neil smiled thinly. "Mike was five or six years old. He couldn't have been Vaughn's."

"What was his father's name? Dallas?"

O'Neil tilted his head. "No . . . I never heard that."

"Well, then, did Vaughn ever say where he met her?"

"No, but it had to be the place he disappeared to those months after he turned twenty-one, didn't it?"

"Most places have names," Dave said.

"All I know is, he was excited because he'd had a chance to do real military training there," O'Neil said. "Combat training. It was brutal, he said. Crawling through the mud, swinging over streams on ropes, climbing cliffs, getting shot at with real ammo. Days all alone being hunted down." O'Neil made a face, drank some of his Coke, laughed sourly. "You should have seen his eyes shine when he told me about it. What a weird kid. It killed him he'd missed Vietnam."

"He missed the Wehrmacht too," Dave said. "But he tried—got expelled from college for painting swastikas."

"Steve admitted that, did he? I'm surprised."

Dave went to find cigarettes and lighter in his desk. "He claims the campus police were malicious, but Steve's lawyers got Vaughn off. Vaughn couldn't be anti-Semitic. Half the Thomas's friends are Jews. Sylvia is Jewish."

"Yeah, well," O'Neil said, "that's a story in itself. Vaughn didn't know from Jewish when Steve married her—he was only eight. But he hated her from the start, nobody could take his mother's place, and later, in junior high school, little Vaughn got caught vandalizing a Jewish cemetery. I'll bet Steve didn't fill you in on that, did he?"

"Tipping over tombstones?" Dave said.

O'Neil nodded. "And painting the walls with yellow six-pointed stars." He tilted the glass up, drained it, ice cubes rattling. "Poor Sylvia." He filled the glass again, the soda fizzing. "And Steve claims she was a wicked stepmother. Claims she hated Vaughn."

Dave drank from his orange juice. "She didn't?"

"It was the other way around, isn't that obvious? But he was a child, Sylvia was an adult. She was patient and understanding and smiled and tried to win him over, didn't she? Baked cookies for him, took him to Knott's, Disneyland, Sea World. Wore herself out. Hell, Mr. Brandstetter, he wouldn't have had any parenting at all if it wasn't for Syl. Sylvia. Mrs. Thomas, I mean. Old Steve had plenty of time and charm to strew around among his clients, but he could forget about Vaughn for months on end. The kid needed him. Wasn't that why he did the rotten things he did? To try to attract his dad's attention?"

"I don't subscribe to *Psychology Today*," Dave said. "In my experience, some people just turn rotten early, Neil. It's how they are."

"I took a minute at lunchtime to check you out. And you're very, very big time." O'Neil's eyes narrowed. "Why are you investigating Vaughn's death? He wasn't at Channel Three long enough to qualify for group insurance."

"Right." Dave smiled. "I figured you were too shrewd to believe that for long."

O'Neil scowled. "You lied? Why? Who for?"

"For someone who doesn't accept that Vaughn's death was an accident. I can't give you my client's name. That's confidential. But I'm sure it would surprise you." Dave grinned. "I know damned well it would surprise Vaughn."

O'Neil stared for a long moment, puzzled, wary. He was pale. He read his watch, set down his glass so hastily it almost fell over. He grabbed for it, straightened it, stood up. "I have to go. Sylvia expects me back tonight." He tried for a smile and missed, then went away down the room at a run. The door that had stood open slammed after him.

Dave plugged in the telephone on the desk and it rang.

"We gave that apartment a thorough going-over," Joey Samuels said. "We didn't find much. Wornout pantyhose, a plastic tricycle." While the police detective talked, Cecil came in the door. He passed Dave, touching his shoulder, hung his jacket on the hat tree by the bar, got a bottle of Beck's from the refrigerator. Samuels said, "A paintball gun and ammo. The jungle suits they wear to play those action combat games. Boots, helmets, belts."

"A paintball gun," Dave said. "No real guns?"

"He stuck to make-believe—war magazines, you know?"

"What about the mailing labels on the magazines?"

"No good—they didn't come through the mail."

"Telephone bills?" Dave said. "They're helpful."

"They didn't have a telephone," Samuels said. "But all the normal papers—auto registration, bank statements, sales receipts, canceled checks—all those were gone. She must have taken them with her."

"Those big shoulder bags have their uses," Dave said.

"A black transvestite hooker in Hollywood hit me with one once," Samuels said. "I heard bells for a week."

Dave laughed. "Thanks," he said, and hung up.

Cecil sat on a corner of the desk, pointed with the green bottle, and asked, "Who belongs to the attaché case?"

Cecil parked his flame-painted, blue-carpeted, picture-windowed van on a steep, twisty hillside street in Burbank, switched off the engine, switched off the lights. It was quiet here, and dark, untrimmed trees hanging over the narrow, tar-patched paving, screening out the scant street-lighting. Bungalows lurked among the trees, below the road on one side, uphill on the other. Clapboard, some of them, some stucco, none of them new. It wasn't late. The windows glowed. When Dave got out of the van and closed the door, a dog barked somewhere. But no human voices sounded. Everybody was indoors watching television. Cecil climbed out on his side of the van, brought out the attaché case, closed his door. He stood beside Dave, looking down wooden steps that led between thick brush into darkness.

"Looks like he still isn't home," he said.

Dave had tried to telephone Neil O'Neil, at work, at home, and got no answer. He'd heated pastrami, piled it thick on sour rye bread, and they'd eaten supper at the big scoured deal table in the cookshack while they watched Channel Three's six o'clock news. Cecil's segment on the Combat Zone looked good, sounded good. He was pleased with it. Now that he'd been promoted, he was a producer. That meant he was still a field reporter but had to work twice as hard. The pay was better but not two times better. It didn't matter. What mattered was, he was getting somewhere. He was black, and getting somewhere in television. After the news, Dave stretched an arm up for the yellow telephone attached to a cupboard in the cookshack and tried to reach O'Neil again. Still no answer. Now in the dark, standing beside O'Neil's mailbox at the road edge in Burbank, he said, "That's what I was hoping. Come on."

They felt their way down the steps. Their shoes had thick silent soles, but these still crackled leaves now and then and snapped twigs. It wasn't going to disturb O'Neil. But it mustn't disturb the neighbors, either. Dave's foot came down on some kind of big, dry seedpod. It burst with a sharp report. The dog barked again, but no human ear had heard, or if it had, it hadn't roused its owner. They reached a deck fronting the house. Dave dug a penlight out of a jacket pocket and ran its beam quickly along the front of the house. Windows. Darkness beyond them. Cecil went to the end of the deck, turned a corner.

"Here," he whispered.

Dave went to him. There was a door. He reached for his wallet. In the wallet he kept small blades helpful sometimes in opening locks. No wallet. "Damn," he said.

"Ssh," Cecil said. He went along the side of the house. Dave stayed where he was. Then he heard a thump, as if a knee had bumped the wall of the house. He went toward the sound. Cecil had disappeared through a small, high window. His long legs in pale jeans were just vanishing inside. Dave went back to the door, and in a moment locks clicked on its far side and the door swung open. Dave could see Cecil's teeth grinning against the darkness.

"You know the bathroom window's always open."

"But my climbing days are over." Dave stepped inside and closed the door. He went around the room, stumbling into furniture, bruising his shins, knees, thighs, closing curtains. He switched on a lamp. The furniture was rattan and wicker from Pier One. The stereo equipment was elaborate but most of it was just piled on the floor. The television set measured forty inches, a VCR on top of it, stacked with tapes. The room beyond showed drafting tables, with lots of paper and tagboard in big sheets, lots of plastic mounted alphabet strips in every conceivable typeface, thick loose-leaf catalogues, ad layouts hanging off the walls, colored paper samples, T-squares, triangles, French curves. A computer monitor turned them a blank face.

Cecil bent over a low wicker table and turned the pages of an investments magazine. "What are we looking for?"

"We'll know when we find it," Dave said.

"Anything connecting this O'Neil to Vaughn Thomas?"

"That too," Dave said, and went through the dining room/office, pushed a swing door, and switched on a light in the kitchen. It had been handsomely remodeled, central burner deck, ovens mounted in the walls, rows of beautiful hanging pots and pans. But the fridge was full of supermarket frozen dinners. That didn't tell Dave anything useful. He went to a bedroom where the bed awaited making up, the sheets in masculine brown stripes. So why did he smell a feminine perfume? The louvered white doors of a walk-in closet were partway open. He opened them all the way. The perfume gusted out. In the closet hung clothes for a young man, yes, but also a woman's clothes, dresses, blouses, slacks. Not many. Enough for emergencies. All peach color. He turned away, frowned, turned back again, bent, picked up off the closet floor a camouflage coverall. New. Worn maybe once. Combat boots lay on the closet floor too. Also new. A helmet with the usual shield to protect the eyes. He knelt and searched, pushing aside shoes, tennis rackets, Frisbees. No paintball gun. He was poking around the bathroom and finding nothing when a car door closed up on the road. He pulled the closet doors near shut again, pocketed a closeup of O'Neil from among twenty snapshots stuck into the mirror over the dresser, then switched off the light. To Cecil, who was pawing through file drawers in the office, he said, "Let's go—and don't forget the attaché case."

In the broad bed on the sleeping loft, Cecil sat propped against pillows, watching the late news on Channel Three. Beside him, back turned, Dave dozed. The familiar voices of the pretty anchor people scarcely reached him. He was almost asleep. Then he heard a cry. Mr. Kaminsky? He looked wildly around the leafy West L.A. patio. Kaminsky was shouting for help. But where was he? Dave flung off the covers and was on his feet before he realized he was dreaming. Cecil switched off the television set. "Hey. Easy, Dave. What's wrong?"

"Kaminsky." Dave sat on the side of the bed. He was panting. His heart raced. "I dreamed about him."

"You heard his name on the news," Cecil said. "Apartment manager? Where Vaughn Thomas lived? He's dead. Fell from a second-floor balcony tonight, broke his neck."

Dave turned and peered into Cecil's face. "Dead?"

"Police searched the apartment earlier. When they got called tonight, door was open, furniture shifted around. They figure he was straightening up. No one saw him fall."

Dave laughed hopelessly. "Poor Kaminsky. He was so excited about being part of a murder case."

"Was he—part of it, I mean?"

"It surprises hell out of me," Dave said.

4

◆

Enid Saddler washed coffee mugs inside the shacky combined gun rental office, equipment store, and canteen at the Combat Zone. It was early. Dave hadn't been sure the place would be open yet. But in the foggy woods, the far-off voices were calling, the paintball guns were popping. Not many. Not often. But he had rolled the Jaguar in among a half dozen cars and campers parked on the rutted earth near the telephone-pole gate. The smell of coffee reached Dave from yards off. He leaned on the counter and told the skin-and-bones woman, "Good morning."

"Mor-ning." Enid didn't so much say it as sing it. But busy arranging mugs on a tray—each stenciled with a bad drawing of a Green Beret holding his M-16 at the ready in case of a Cong assault—Enid didn't look up for a moment. When she did, the light went out of her eyes. Her voice lost its music. "Oh, it's you again." She was not pleased, but all the same she drew coffee from an immense square-cornered aluminum machine, brought the mug with a spoon and a tiny paper napkin, set it in front of him. "I thought we were finished with that killing business. Police, television. They done their work and says thank you and goodbye, but not you. You're back."

"Just with a quick question." Dave reached for his wallet, remembered, dug in a pocket and took out a fold of bills. He'd borrowed them from Cecil. He laid a one on the counter. "Thank you for the coffee."

She pushed the one back at him. "We don't charge law enforcement officers." She smiled. It was as false as the teeth that made it possible. "What did you want to know?"

Dave tasted the scalding coffee. "Where's Roy?"

"Ailing again," she said grimly. "I don't know how long he's going to last, and that's the truth. Some days he's weak as a baby. That cough. You ever hear Roy cough? Them cigarettes is killing him, but he won't stop."

Dave's hand had moved to his jacket pocket to take out his Marlboros. He didn't complete the action.

"Says it's your time to go, you go." Enid went back to her cramped kitchen and began taking doughnuts from gray, grease-spotted cardboard boxes and stacking them on platters. "Says his Daddy lived to ninety-one and he never saw the man without a cigarette in his life." She brought a platter of doughnuts to the counter. "Try one of these. They're fresh delivered this morning."

"Everybody gets up early around here," he said.

She laughed. Briefly. And her flat eyes stared out at the woods. "I swear, some of them are like children. Can't think of anything but playing paintball. Crack of dawn, they're up and out. Listen, if we put in a restaurant like Roy wants, and showers, and all that, they'll play all night too, I swear they will."

"This one?" Dave pushed the snapshot he'd plucked from O'Neil's bedroom mirror across the counter for her to look at. "Did he ever come here?"

She had powdered sugar on her fingers. She licked them, wiped them on her apron, picked up the photo, and studied it. She shook her head and passed it back to Dave. "Maybe, but you have to understand, they come here with their helmets on, a lot of them with that war paint on their faces, it's hard to tell one from the other." She breathed another of those sharp little laughs of hers. "Boys from the girls, for that matter. And it's only a field to play games in—we don't check IDs. People don't give names. Hell, half that come here

regular, I don't know their last name. Mostly only nicknames—
Gorilla George, Grace the Mace, you know?"

"I do now." He looked at the photo. "Is there a chance you could
show this to Roy? I think this man was here the day Vaughn Thomas
was shot. I'd like a witness."

"I thought you was going to start that up again." Enid's face
closed like a slammed door. She stood rigid, mouth clamped tight.
"That boy was killed by a stray bullet and it didn't come from here.
We don't use bullets." She marched off, reached up to a shelf,
returned with a colorful carton that she opened. From it she brought
a long plastic tube. "These are what we use. Balls made of gelatin
with washable paint inside. Couldn't kill anybody."

"I'm aware of that. But you don't have security here. And the
paintball guns I saw yesterday, and the ones hanging up there behind
you—some of them are made to look like assault rifles, AK-47s,
Uzis, AR-15s, Galils, Steyr AUGs. On purpose. To add realism to
the games."

She stared at him icily. "That's right."

"So do you think you or Roy would notice if instead of a paintball
imitation, this fellow"—Dave flicked the edge of O'Neil's photo
with a fingernail—"were to walk in here with the real thing?"

"It was a deer hunter's bullet," she said sullenly.

"It blew half his head away," Dave said, "and went right on into
these woods. The police don't know the exact kind of bullet it was."

"You going to drink that coffee or not?"

"I'll drink it," Dave said, "while you show this to Roy, please."
He held out the photo. "Don't worry, I'll tell anyone that comes
you'll be right back." She stood uncertain. "Please? To help a law
enforcement officer?"

She snatched the photo and marched off with it. Dave lit a cigarette
and worked on the coffee. Enid didn't have to worry. She could
always open an eatery. It was wonderful coffee. Or maybe it tasted
so good because he was drinking it outdoors in early morning country
air. Anyway, for a few minutes, he was happy. Then Enid came
back, Roy trailing behind her, whiskery, tucking shirttails into his

pants, shuffling in untied shoes. He grunted at Dave, drew coffee from the machine, came to the counter with it, laid the picture down, and shook his head.

"He didn't come with Vaughn Thomas that day?"

"They know each other?" Roy said, and coughed, and fumbled a cigarette out of his shirt pocket, and lit it with a kitchen match, and coughed again. These weren't serious coughs. He didn't appear to have strength enough for those.

"Worked together for a while," Dave said.

Roy burned himself on the hot coffee and said, "Shit." He fixed the cigarette in a corner of his mouth, picked up the photo and squinted at it again, then held it out in a shaky hand for Dave to take back. "Nope. Don't place the face. Anyways, I told you, Vaughn always come alone. A loner. Ask around here. They'll all tell you the same."

"The Channel Three reporter is a friend of mine," Dave said. "He asked around. They said what you said."

"A friend of yours?" Roy blinked. "The nigger kid?"

"We live together," Dave said.

Roy turned. "Enid, did you ever hear the like of that?"

Dave backed the Jaguar from among the other cars, shifted gears, was moving for the gate, when a rusty pickup truck with a camper on the back barged through, kicking up dust. Dave braked. The pickup missed him by an inch and rattled to a halt. The man who got out of the pickup didn't so much as glance Dave's way. Dressed in camouflage with the sleeves rolled up, a brown beret tilted on his long yellow hair, he locked the truck's cab, tramped around to open the camper, reached inside, and brought out ammunition belts. He hung these all over himself, then leaned in and came out with an armload of guns. He was very tall, and his long arms managed the guns easily. He used a knee to slam the door of the camper, then headed for the Combat Zone's all-purpose shack.

On the rear bumper of the pickup Dave saw a ragged, faded

bumper sticker—a stylized double lightning bolt. The mark of Hitler's Waffen SS troops. Dave had gone into Germany as a U.S. Army intelligence lieutenant just after the surrender. He knew that mark well. It was among the ugliest symbols of a nightmare time. A classy crowd Roy Saddler drew here. Dave watched from the Jaguar while the tall type paid his tariff, got a mug of coffee and half a dozen doughnuts, and sat on a log to eat. From the woods appeared a plump girl whose outfit was splashed with paint. She sat down beside him on the log, laid her gun across her knees, and told him how it happened, with flying gestures and shrill laughter. He grinned and wagged his head.

Now another vehicle came tearing between the telephone poles. This was a dusty white van, an old VW, and out of it jumped four more camouflaged and combat-booted young people. They cheered when they saw the tall one on the log. He gave them a doughnut-filled grin and a wave. They slammed the van doors and ran to him. Dave eased the Jaguar back again into the parking place he'd left, switched off the engine, set the parking brake, and sat quietly watching while the newcomers got coffee and sat on the log, on rocks, on the ground, loading the paintball guns the tall one supplied, and talking and joking and making plans for the game. They were many yards distant, so the words didn't reach him, just the voices. He wasn't interested in the words. He was interested in the tall brute. Kaminsky's word for him—if this was him. *Long hair—looked like he came out of the backwoods someplace.*

When at last he rose and led his troops into the fog-bound trees, Dave got out of the Jaguar. He glanced through the dusty, rain-spotted windows of the camper as he passed. Just glanced. His actions could be seen from the canteen. Sunlight so fell through windows on the other side of the camper that they lit up two rectangles that showed Dave guns. He didn't dare pause to make sure, but he judged these were not paintball guns—and a coldness formed in the pit of his stomach. He hadn't brought his Sig Sauer 9mm pistol. It was at home, in a dresser drawer up on the sleeping loft. He had a gift for forgetting it. Carefully not looking toward the service window, he trudged around the canteen's far end. He'd seen doors there when he was here before, doors with rustically carved signs MEN, WOMEN. He pushed inside, used the urinal, rinsed and dried his hands, came out, and the plump young woman bumped into him.

"Hey," she said, looking him up and down, "sorry."

"No harm," Dave said, and smiled.

Her face was smeared with camouflage paint. She looked like a fat boy of thirteen. Dave stepped aside. She stepped aside in the same direction. She laughed. He didn't laugh. "The tall fellow you were talking to. Is his name Dallas, by any chance?"

"Yeah," she said, "he's a fixture here." Frowning, she looked Dave's handwoven tweeds over doubtfully again. "You want me to introduce you?"

"I just need to know his last name." Dave showed her his license. "It's an insurance matter."

"He don't need insurance." She glanced toward the woods, which were much noisier now, shouts, crashing underbrush, guns popping wildly. "He can look after himself."

"I don't sell it," Dave said. "I'm handling a liability claim. He's a witness, that's all."

"Yeah?" she said. "Car crash or something?"

Dave nodded. "His last name?"

"We don't go by last names," she said, and held out her hand. "I'm Maxine. Max the Ax."

Dave shook the hand. "I won't bother him today. Where does he live?"

"At the beach someplace." She shrugged and wrinkled her childish brow. "Cormorant Cove?"

Film people, television people, rock stars, recording executives lived in Cormorant Cove. If you didn't have three or four million dollars to spend on housing, real estate people didn't take you there. Of course, what Ngawi Smith said was true—drug dealers, money launderers, video pirates looked like anybody else. They could afford to live in Cormorant Cove. Hell, they could buy out Cormorant Cove. Maybe they had. Maybe that made plausible what Max the Ax said, that Dallas lived there. No matter how corrupt your business, if it's any size, you need hired hands.

"Cormorant Cove," Dave said. "Good." He looked at his watch. "I have to run. Nice to meet you, Max." He walked away, with a lift of his hand. "Thank you for your help."

"You want me to tell him you asked for him?" she called.

"Don't bother," Dave said. "He doesn't know me."

The road from the Combat Zone was a basic two-lane strip of pitted asphalt that sloped down through foothills, not twenty yards of it in a straight line. All land falling away on this side, rising on that. Where it met the highway was a cluster of houses and stores called Delmore Pass. He pulled into a filling station and used coins on the pay phone there. The idea of slipping a credit card into a phone hadn't got as far as Delmore Pass yet. It took a half hour of trying, but at last he reached Joey Samuels at LAPD homicide division. He recited the license number of Dallas's truck.

"It'll take a few minutes," Samuels said. "Lots of checking going on this morning. Give me the number where you are, and I'll get back to you."

"Thanks, Joey." Dave gave him the number, hung the gritty gray receiver back in place, went and put gas into the Jaguar, stepped into the sheet-metal office. It was a surprising place. Books and magazines stacked everywhere. The attendant was a man so fat he didn't try to get out of his chair, a recliner with splits in its leather. He had a cash register and a credit card gizmo and all else on a level where he could reach them from a sitting position. The man wheezed with every breath. His words came out as gasps. He fiddled with slips of paper and Dave's card. His hands were swollen with fat. It was some kind of miracle that he could do anything with his fingers, but he did, and handed Dave his receipt with his card.

"You been up to the Combat Zone," he said. "Twice."

"Just visiting." Dave signed the credit card papers.

"You don't look like you'd play action pursuit," the man said. "Mostly it's kids in their twenties. Then there's a few Vietnam veterans, didn't get it out of their system. Nostalgia, maybe, wanting to be young again."

"But all of them white—yes?" Dave said.

The man's features were all bunched together in the middle of his bloated face. He blinked, considering the question. At last he said, "Disproportionately high number of blacks in the U.S. armed forces. But you never see them going up the road to the Combat Zone."

"I didn't think so," Dave said.

The man snorted. "You ever meet Roy Saddler?"

"That's why I asked," Dave said.

"I was hoping his business was so poor he'd soon move on," the fat man said. "I don't want to be a neighbor to people like that—bigots. But now that that boy was shot to death up there, I fear good old Roy will be here till I die. The TV news will send curiosity seekers flocking up here."

"Roy was counting on it," Dave said, "but so far it doesn't seem to be happening."

The fat man wheezed a laugh and raised his eyes to look at a clock that bore the red-white-and-blue insignia of an oil company on its face. "Hell, it's early yet. Not even eight o'clock. They'll be along, I promise you." He pawed around beside his chair and came up with a brightly striped, crackly plastic sack. He held it out. "Chocolate chip?"

Dave smiled, shook his head. "It's too early for me."

The fat man laughed, pushed a cookie into his mouth, laid the package in his lap. Spraying crumbs, he said, "You'll see. People just can't stay away from the scene of a calamity. You can hear every morning on the radio how they jam up the freeways slowing down to gawk at a crash. Nothing like the misfortunes of others to set us staring."

"It won't bother the dead boy," Dave said.

"No, that's true enough," the fat man said, and poked another cookie into his mouth.

"And if it's good for Roy Saddler's business," Dave said, "it's surely going to be good for yours."

The fat man opened his eyes wide. "By golly," he puffed. "You're right there. That's life. 'In time of plague, the undertaker prospers.' "

"Did you know the boy?" Dave said. "Vaughn Thomas?"

The man turned glum suddenly. "He stopped here once. Sneery kind of a kid. Didn't say it to my face, but walking back to his car, after he paid me, he says as if he's talking to himself, 'Sooee, sooee, sooee, pig, pig, pig.' "

"You're not mourning for him, then?" Dave said.

The fat man smiled wanly. "I mourn for all who lose their lives. Life is all we've got. He was young. He might have grown wiser and kinder—if he'd had time."

Outside, the pay phone began ringing. No mistake. The bell was as loud as a burglar alarm. "Excuse me," Dave said. The fat man didn't answer. He had already picked up a book, opened it, and was reading, totally absorbed. Dave crunched across gravel to the phone, lifted down the receiver. "Brandstetter," he said.

"It's a 1972 GM," Samuels said, "registered to Dallas Eric Engstrom, two seven zero Lemon Street, Winter Creek."

"He doesn't live there anymore," Dave said. "I'm told his new address is in Cormorant Cove."

"I haven't got anything on that," Samuels said. "You'll have to get it from the phone company."

"Thanks," Dave said. "I'll try."

But if Dallas Engstrom answered a phone in Cormorant Cove or in any nearby beach town, the phone wasn't his. Dave returned to the Jaguar. Time was nagging at him. If Dallas and Jemmie had been husband and wife, Jemmie probably came from Winter Creek too. He knew the town. He'd worked on a case there, how long ago now, thirty years? Spent almost two weeks getting to the bottom of it. A sluttish woman's sixteen-year-old son, in a mixture of outraged love and fury at her whoring, had knocked her senseless, driven the car to a deep ravine, put her behind the wheel, sent the car over a cliff.

Winter Creek hadn't liked Dave for turning up the truth. It was a small town in 1960. It wouldn't have stayed that way—no place in California had. But it shouldn't be hard to find Jemmie's father who bred horses. Then again, what if homesick Ngawi Smith was wrong—and she hadn't gone to ground at her parents' place? He shrugged impatiently. It was no good worrying about details now.

He started the Jaguar. He could be in Winter Creek by ten-thirty. He was a mile down the highway when he scowled, drove onto the shoulder, and stopped. He really was getting old. He'd forgotten Dallas. Jemmie was far away. And maybe she was safe there. She thought she would be—and she knew more about it than Dave did. Jemmie was not in his hands. Dallas was. And why wasn't Dallas the killer Jemmie had looked for so worriedly out the back window of Smith's cab on the way to the bus station? Max the Ax would be sure to tell Dallas Dave was looking for him. It should flush him out of the woods. Dave made a U-turn on the empty pavement, drove back to where the side road met the highway, parked in brush behind the raw plank COMBAT ZONE sign, and waited.

5

◆

Cormorant Cove was built in shelves on sharply rising hills above a deep, round, inward curve of beach. A few little shallow-draft sailboats lay on the sand. Jagged black rocks poked up in the small, blue bay. The tide splashed and foamed around the rocks. Cormorants had been scarce on this stretch of coast when Dave used to come here, years before there'd been any houses. Then DDT was outlawed, and slowly the cormorants came back. A flock of them perched lean and beaky and black on the black rocks now, holding out their wings to take the morning sun.

The houses here were big and most of them no more than ten years old, a few sensible frame-and-shingle, like beach houses anywhere ought to be, but most pretentious, sterile, white modifications of the Mediterranean. They looked cold as refrigerators. It was in at the drive of one of these, three tiers up from the beach, that Dallas Engstrom swung his clanky pickup. Dave rolled to curbside up the block. Signs corroded by salt air told him parking wasn't allowed here. It made sense. The curved streets were too narrow. But he had no choice.

He ambled down the road, gazing at the sand and surf below, and stopped opposite the garage, where a quick glance showed him Engstrom had left his truck beside a gleaming Rolls-Royce Silver Cloud. They made an incongruous pair. It was a triple garage. Dave wondered what the other car was. Engstrom was climbing stairs. Dave's ears told him that. He chanced another glance over his shoulder. A staircase mounted the outside of the garage. At its top, Engstrom unlocked and went through a door. Into a chauffeur's quarters? It seemed a fair guess. A shower, shave, change of clothes would take him fifteen minutes.

Dave wandered on down the road, around the next curve, out of sight, stood and watched the water dash against the rocks and send up spray, creep up the sand, turning it dark for a moment. Shore birds stilted along the tide's edge, stitching the sand, hurrying on. He kept checking his watch. At the end of fifteen minutes, he ambled back the way he had come. In time to see Engstrom, now wearing a white houseman's jacket and trousers, very starchy clean, go along a narrow passageway and disappear around a rear corner of the house. Dave crossed the narrow road and followed him.

Through a barred black metal screen door came cooking smells. Dave rapped the door. In a minute Engstrom stood there, looking taller close up. "You were at the fields," he said, more than a hint of country in his speech. "What did you do—follow me from there? Max says you was asking about me. Who are you? What do you want?"

Dave gave his name, took out his license in its ostrich-hide folder, dropped it open though no one could read it against the light through that tough security screen. "I'm a private investigator looking into the shooting death of Vaughn Thomas."

Dallas made a noise that was not speech.

"You knew he was killed at the Combat Zone, Sunday?"

"Killed? Vaughn? Christ, no." Dallas shook his head. "At the fields? Nobody said nothing to me about it."

"It was on the news," Dave said.

"I watch basketball," Dallas said. He grinned, he almost chuckled. "So somebody snuffed the little bastard."

"We have to talk," Dave said. "I need to come in."

"What for? I got work to do."

"He stole your wife," Dave said. "You hated him. You went to his apartment in L.A. and threw him down the stairs. You tried to talk Jemmie into coming back to you. When she wouldn't, you tried it out on little Mike. Now I find you play war games at the Combat Zone, just like Vaughn. I think those are good reasons for us to talk, don't you?"

Engstrom hesitated, rocking on his long legs, looking ferocious. But at last he unlatched the screen and pushed it open. "All right," he growled. "You got it all wrong. I can see that. Come on in." Dave stepped into a big kitchen where three brown, underweight Asian men, wrapped in white aprons, worked at high-flame burners and at long counters. The air was keen with smells of crab, lobster, shrimp. "Damn Swanhilde ain't here, anyway," Engstrom grouched. " 'Get back before noon, Dallas,' she says, 'or I'll cut you down to fit Danny DeVito's wardrobe, darling.' " Dallas led the way out of the kitchen, down a long white hallway, and out onto a broad white terrace that faced the ocean. "And where the fuck is she? A note? A message with the slants? Forget it. I hope the fucking paparazzi blind her with their strobes." He dragged lacy white wrought-iron chairs to the railed edge of the terrace. "Sit down."

Dave sat. "Were you at the fields Sunday morning?"

Dallas, a long brown cigarette in the corner of his mouth, and using a big, clean workman's hand to shield the flame of a battered Zippo lighter from the sea breeze, stared at Dave. "You think I killed him?"

"Somebody who knew how to make it to look like an accident, somebody familiar with the place, somebody who owns a high-powered gun. You wanted your wife and son back. Maybe you figured with him out of the way, that would happen."

"Jesus." Engstrom got the light for his cigarette and clapped shut the top of the Zippo. "Doesn't it bother you, sneaking around nosing into people's private business?" He eyed Dave with distaste while the sea breeze made thin shreds of his cigarette smoke. "It makes me sick. Somebody's watching. Somebody's listening. This used to be a free country. I bled for this country in Nam, two goddamn tours, and I get treated like a fucking criminal."

"Where were you Sunday morning?" Dave said again.

"Right the hell here," Engstrom shouted. He waved a hand to take in beach, sky, terrace, house, all. "You can ask Sampan or whatever his name is in the kitchen. His people got lost trying to find the place. He had me up at six A.M. to help him. And I mean, there wasn't time to take a leak, for Christ sake. A hundred people coming"—the watch he looked at was a very old underwater model, heavy enough to fell a man at a single blow—"like today. I didn't only have to do half the kitchen work, when I can't understand ninety percent of the directions the son of a bitch was giving me, I had to do all the setting up out here. Including the fucking flowers."

"And after that you served the drinks," Dave said.

"Damn right." Engstrom nodded. A white headband held his hair, but its long ends blew in the breeze. "Until the last sitcom star cleared off in his Mercedes at close to two. He was figuring on climbing into bed with Swanhilde. She picked him up and held him out the window up there." He pointed at the high white face of the house. "Squealed like a pig, stupid midget." He laughed sourly. "Ask Jeffie Strickland if I was here."

"You never ran into Vaughn Thomas at the Combat Zone?"

"If I had," Engstrom said, "I'd have tied him to a tree. By his neck." He stopped himself, red-faced. "Forget I said that. No, I never knew he went there. Ask me, I'd have told you he was finished with war games."

Dave said, "Where did you meet him?"

"Winter Creek," Engstrom said sulkily. "He shows up one day in this fucking top-down little red Italian sports car, asking the way to George Hetzel's."

Dave had heard the name. In what connection? Something unpleasant. He waited.

"He'd read about Hetzel in *Soldier of Fortune* magazine or one of those," Engstrom said, "and he was down here to take training. Hetzel's got a hundred twenty acres of fields, woods, ravines, rivers."

"But not like the Combat Zone," Dave said. "Not for recreation."

Engstrom waved a dismissive hand. "Hell, no. Hetzel is serious. He runs full training programs in commando tactics, guerrilla warfare, jungle crawling, the works. Real bullets, grenades, booby traps, mortars, even a mine field. He wants to give this country back to the white people."

Now Dave remembered the man. He'd been Grand Dragon of the California Ku Klux Klan. Then he'd made a run for State Assembly and missed. Now he was mustering skinheads, white suburban teenage boys whose specialty was kicking and stomping with steel-toed shoes Jews, blacks, Mexican illegals, homosexuals—the list was long. Dave looked out at the glittering bay. "And Vaughn Thomas wanted to be part of it?"

"Five thousand dollars worth," Engstrom snorted. "Was a time you had to be a man to get in. But Hetzel—I guess all the publicity—*Time, Newsweek, Rolling Stone*—went to his head. He's turning just like the rest of the country. Money and fame is all that matters."

"Vaughn gave him five thousand dollars for a few weeks' military training? He could have had it free in the marines. And better too, probably."

"Not and been a major soon as Hetzel inducted him." Engstrom snorted again. "Shit. You ever hear anything so disgusting? You ever see Vaughn Thomas? Frail as a goddamn girl. He couldn't do any of it. None of it. Everything he tried he fell off of or tripped over. He was a joke. Everybody was laughing at him. He complained, and Hetzel cracked down, and after that he got the idea he was top dog. No shit."

"You were in Hetzel's band of merry men?" Dave said.

"One of the first," Engstrom said proudly, "years ago, when he was just starting up. I came back from Nam, and he grabbed me right away. I was with him a long time. Me and my buddy, Barney Craig. Then he threw me out. I got in a scrape, barroom fight"— Engstrom's big square shoulders rose and fell—"no big deal. But a month in jail went with it, and he said it was bad for the Movement's image, and I was out. 'Image.' " Engstrom snorted. "You should have seen his face when he said it. Looked like a fucking Sunday school teacher. I couldn't believe he was serious. I was the best instructor he had. After that, he reorganized the whole show army style, by the book, with Barney as his aide de camp."

Dave raised an eyebrow. "Not Vaughn Thomas?"

"This was years before he showed up," Engstrom said, then half grinned. "But if he'd been there then with his stinking five thousand bucks, you're probably right."

"So you weren't in Hetzel's outfit when Thomas came?"

"Naw, but Barney told me about it. We was still friends, then, partners. After Nam, we'd set up in the construction business. Not contractors—journeymen, all right? Down in Winter Creek, it amounts to the same thing. Somebody wanted something built or added onto or even just fixed up—you call Dallas and Barney. Bricklaying, welding, carpentry, electricity, poured concrete—we did it all."

"And you still had time for Hetzel's outfit?"

"Wasn't a lot to it, then." Engstrom watched two of the Asians from the kitchen come onto the terrace with loads of tablecloths and napkins. They dusted off the tables, and working as a team because of the wind, covered the tables, folded the napkins so they'd stand up with neat points, and arranged the napkins on the cloths. "We passed a lot of time over at Del Mar at the races, down to San Diego for the Padres games. Nights we whooped it up in taverns." Now the third Asian wheeled a steel cart onto the terrace. On its shelves bottles and glasses jingled. He set the bottles out on a long table. He made three circular clusters of sparkling wine, highball, and cocktail glasses. Engstrom sighed. "Then it changed. Barney got to hanging around more and more with Clarice from the Twin Oaks Café, and after that, things was never the same. I seemed to be alone pretty much of the time."

"And this was when you met Jemmie?" Dave said.

"Her old man, Charlie Pratt, breeds horses. Nice stock. He used to be a jockey, but not the kind that makes millions, so when he broke his pelvis for the last time and had to retire, he couldn't afford thoroughbreds, of course. No buyers for thoroughbreds in Winter Creek anyways. But last six, seven years well-heeled people started moving down to Winter Creek, away from L.A.—the drugs, the gangs, the niggers, and the rest of it—and one of the things they hanker for is to own a couple horses, or their kids hanker for horses, right? So business was good for old Charlie, and he asked Barney and me to build him another stable. And when we was working on it, that's when I met Jemmie."

"And you got married, and had little Mike, and——"

Engstrom held up a hand. "Whoa. First place, old man Pratt, soon as he saw how it was between us he told Jemmie no way was she to have anything to do with me. I was trash, a jailbird and a drunk. Worse than that, I was one of Hetzel's bunch—and Pratt's a communist."

"Seriously?" Dave said.

"You better believe it. All the time weeping over what Hitler done to the Jews, and how the nation owes it to the niggers to see to it they get an even break, and— oh, I don't want to repeat it. Makes me sick." Engstrom pushed angrily to his feet. "You want a drink? That's what I'm here for, you know—make the guests comfortable."

Dave read his watch. Too early. "I'll pass, thanks. Pratt objected, but you did get married."

"He had a shotgun and a bad temper." Engstrom went off along the terrace to the drinks table and came back with a bottle of Perrier water. He pried the cap off with his thumb and drank. "I took him serious. Didn't even look at Jemmie for a week, maybe more. Then one night away late, she's at my door, crying and begging and carrying on. 'Let's go to Vegas and get married,' she says. 'I can't stand life without you no more, Dallas,' and you know how girls talk, and I'd had about eight beers, and I says, 'What the hell— why not?' "

"And Pratt didn't make any trouble?" Dave said.

"I had sheriffs and lawyers and judges up the ass." Engstrom laughed. "I figured I'd get three life sentences to San Quentin, the way he took after me. Went on for weeks—I never laid eyes on Jemmie, all that time. He wouldn't let her out of the house. But then she come up pregnant. And you wouldn't believe the change in the mean old bastard. Overnight. I don't mean he was nice to me. But he laid off with the law, and he let her move in with me. Really, Jemmie was the one who was sore. When Mike was born, I says to her she ought to make it up with old Charlie—he'd want to see his grand-son, he'd be proud."

"And?" Dave said.

Engstrom thrust out his lower lip, shook his head. "She was as good a hater as he was. No way. Never talked to him from that day till this one."

"How did she meet Vaughn?" Dave said.

Engstrom turned the little green bottle in his long, knuckly fingers. His mouth twitched bitterly. "Hetzel got this campaign going against a low-cost housing development going up in Winter Creek. Government-funded. Too much affluence. No houses for low-income people. Meaning niggers, of course. Hetzel got on the public access television in Fortuna just about every day, talking against it. Meetings, rallies up and down the county. He got up a petition to send to Sacramento. Had everybody he could find going from door to door, trying to get people to sign their name on it. And mailings. You never seen anything like it. Well, he needed office help, and Barney told Jemmie, and Mike wasn't so little anymore, and she'd go in and stuff envelopes. George paid her. That's mostly why she did it. We was broke."

"What happened to the contracting business?"

"Barney got busier and busier with Hetzel," Engstrom said, "and I couldn't handle it alone. Naw, truth is"—he looked ashamed, turned his head aside—"I'd found out there was an easier way to make money." He stopped talking.

"And how's that?" Dave prompted.

"Movies," Engstrom said, and looked at him again, with a wry smile. "Company come down to Winter Creek to do some location shooting, and they hired me and twenty others to be 'atmosphere people.' You ever hear of that?"

"I've heard of it," Dave said.

"I never did. And shit, they paid. Day after day. They paid me wild money for sitting on a bar stool with a glass of beer and a bowl of peanuts and a pack of cigarettes and wearing a cowboy hat on the back of my head. Shit."

"So you thought you'd go to Hollywood?" Dave said.

Engstrom nodded, disgustedly. "Couldn't think about nothing else—sure as hell not about installing eighty toilets in a housing tract at Lizard Rocks. See—" He leaned toward Dave, an earnest hand held out. "This producer, Lyman Katz, he tells me I'm a standout. I'm photo hygienic, all right? I'm big and rugged and sexy, okay, I'm another Nick Nolte? And if I ever come to L.A., look him up—this Lyman Katz, I mean. So I wasn't working. I was laying around the house dreaming about being a movie star. And Jemmie went to earn a few bucks from Hetzel to buy groceries with." Engstrom shook his head. "What a jackass I was."

"And she met Vaughn Thomas at Hetzel's?"

"Strutting around like a little rooster, with all these guns strapped to him," Engstrom said, "and bragging how rich he was, how his old man owns this big business in L.A., and how little Vaughn is going to inherit it all and give it to Hetzel for ARAMMO—the Aryan America Movement."

"Why didn't you break it up?" Dave said. "You're certainly bigger and stronger than he was."

"I tried. I knew something was going on. Only I had the wrong dude. I thought it was Barney Craig. He and Clarice had broke up, and I thought he was making out with Jemmie, and I got drunk one night and beat the shit out of Barney at the Old Corral, and then I came home and tried to beat up Jemmie. Only I passed out after about one wild swing, and she took little Mike and ran to Hetzel's, and when I woke up the next morning they was gone. Her and Mike and Vaughn. Hetzel was mad as hell. He's a man looks cool all the time, acts cool all the time, but it's banked fires with old George, you bet. He's a wounded bear when he gets mad. Makes your skin crawl."

"You figured they'd come to L.A.," Dave said, "and you came after them?"

Engstrom nodded glumly. "Couldn't find them, though, could I? Shit, there's about ten thousand Thomases in the phone book. This is a big—I mean B-I-G"—he wrote the letters in the air—"town. I finally looked up Lyman Katz and says, 'Here I am. I decided to take you up on your offer.' I could see he never expected to see me again, but he asks me in for a drink, and says things are slow right now, sorry. Hell, I'm broke. Does he offer me a loan? No way. But he needs help with the house. It's huge. In the Hollywood Hills. So what the hell, I'm his houseman, okay? Then somebody breaks in and steals everything, and guess what? Katz tells the police it was me. It wasn't me, and he knows it, but he was protecting his cocaine supplier."

"I read about this," Dave said. "I thought your name was familiar. The case against you was dismissed."

"Not before I spent a week in jail," Engstrom said. "I'd still be there, but they found the stuff that was stole and busted the Colombian sucker that took it."

"And that ended your movie career?" Dave said.

"So far," Engstrom said. "But I'm doing all right." He smirked. "Swanhilde thinks I'm better than Nick Nolte. She pays me five hundred a week to put on a tuxedo and drive her places and push the photographers off, or get into a white jacket and buzz around with drinks and food at parties. But I sleep a lot"—he wiggled his brows—"and not alone. Every man in America wants to sleep where I sleep."

The sound of car doors closing out on the street, happy cries of greeting drifted out to the terrace. Dave wondered who in the world Swanhilde was. He'd have to ask Cecil.

"You did find Vaughn," he said. "How?"

"When I walked out of jail that morning, I stood on the sidewalk taking big breaths of air, to get the stink of the place out of my lungs. And there, right across the street, Jemmie comes out of the Hall of Records. She walks to the curb and stands looking at the cars. She's waiting to be picked up, right? I'm ready to dodge across the street against the light, but the traffic's too heavy and moving too fast. Then Vaughn rolls up in that red sports car of his, and she gets in, and they drive away."

From beyond the open French doors to the terrace came sounds of shoes on stairs, echoing conversation, too bright, too high-pitched, ricochets of merriment.

Engstrom went on. "I flagged a taxi and followed them home. I wanted to talk to Jemmie, apologize to her for not working, drinking all day, getting mean with her—tell her I want her back, her and Mike, the way we was before. But not with Vaughn there. I'd go back the next day."

"Only Vaughn was still there," Dave said. "You had a fight with him, and the apartment manager threatened to call the police and you ran off. But you came back and hung around the neighborhood when you could. You talked to little Mike. What about last night? Did you go again last night?"

Engstrom squinted. "Last night—hell no. Why?"

"Somebody went through that apartment, shoving furniture around. Somebody pushed the apartment manager off the balcony. Killed him. I figure you could do both."

"I was here last night," Engstrom said, "watching TV in my room. I went to bed early so's to get up early."

"Can you prove it?" Dave said.

"Can you prove I wasn't?" Engstrom said.

Well-dressed people, smiling, suntanned, most of them in dark glasses, began to come out onto the terrace.

"What was she doing at the Hall of Records?" Dave said.

Engstrom made a face. "Filing for divorce."

"She told you that? At the apartment that day?"

"First thing out of her mouth," Engstrom said. "We was through, it was all over, she was getting a divorce, and she never wanted to see me or talk to me again." He blew out air, gloomily, then suddenly stood up. "Jesus. Vaughn's out of the way, now. I ought to go to her." He gazed unhappily at the gathering party crowd. "Shit— wouldn't you know?" His eyes begged Dave. "Can you go there, tell her I'm coming?"

Dave said, "She's not there. She's run away, Dallas."

"No." He paled. His eyes narrowed. "Jesus—where to?"

"I thought you might be able to tell me."

"Shit—I don't know." He held his arms out, helplessly, and let them drop. "I suppose Winter Creek, wouldn't she? I mean, it's where she was raised, went to school, all that. Winter Creek's all she knows."

"You say she and her father are estranged," Dave said. "Has she any other family?"

"Not family. She might go to Barney—only I don't guess so, now that him and Clarice broke up." Engstrom's low brow wrinkled. "Who else—Hetzel? No—I don't know." He waved distractedly at some party guests, flashed them a grin, and scowled at Dave. "What do you want with her?"

"She knows who killed Vaughn, or she knows why he was killed, and in either case she's in danger."

"I'll go." Engstrom set the bottle on the terrace rail. "She's still my wife. It's my job to protect her." He loped off. Dave went after him, against the incoming tide of new arrivals. A glorious tall blonde in white chiffon swept past, white-gloved arms raised, and braying for attention.

Swanhilde? He caught up to her. "Excuse me." She stopped and stared, at first coldly, then with a hint of warmth. He didn't know what it meant, but while he had her attention he gave his name, showed his license, and told a half truth. "I'm looking into a missing persons matter. Your houseman, Dallas Engstrom, may be a witness. Now, he tells me he was busy here last Sunday. Helping the caterer. You had a party. Is he remembering correctly?"

"There's nothing wrong with his memory." She laughed and turned away. "But he's a little weak on truth-telling." Her amazing cobalt blue eyes studied Dave again. As if he were edible. "The party was on a Sunday, all right, but not last Sunday. It was the Sunday before, Mr. —"

"Brandstetter," he said.

"Brandstetter." She smiled again, touched her lips with her tongue, and winked. "I'll remember that." Then she was off, shouting, "Dallas, where's the fucking quartet?"

6

◆

Laurel Canyon Boulevard climbs and does a lot of bending too—like the road to the Combat Zone. But though it's not that much wider, it's a hell of a lot busier, and the traffic held his attention. He was trying to move fast, without success. He had to figure Dallas Engstrom, not a regular commuter to Los Angeles, would take the obvious route to Winter Creek—the San Diego Freeway, busiest of them all, where traffic often slowed to a crawl, sometimes halted altogether. Dave remembered back roads that would cut forty-five, fifty minutes off the time. He didn't want to lose that advantage by stopping at home, but it couldn't be helped.

He had swung in at Horseshoe Canyon Trail, shifted into first, and set the Jaguar nosing upward when he saw the flash of yellow surfer trunks at a crossroads. He braked the Jaguar so the tires squealed. He pulled the car onto a tilted road shoulder, killed the engine, yanked the brake, jumped out. "Hey," he shouted, and ran down the road toward the kid, who threw him a startled look, saw who he was, turned, and took to his dirty naked heels, not down the road, but through brushy yards, tree-grown vacant lots, into a ravine thick with scrub oak, pine, and fern. He was gone in seconds. Dave stood panting on the wooden walk to somebody's house, unsound in wind and limb, too old to follow.

Minutes later, he eased the car down into the brick yard where

Cecil's van stood nearest the French windows of the front building. He pulled in beside it, hurried around the shingled end to cross the patio, and found Cecil sitting on the bench that clasped the oak. He sat bent double, arms folded across his flat belly. Dave went to him, crouched, touched his hanging head.

"What's wrong? Shall I call an ambulance?"

"No." Cecil groaned and shook his head miserably. "Son of a bitch." He lifted his head, grimacing. "Street kids. Been away too long. I wasn't ready. Kicked me right in the balls. Oh, shit. I liked to die here."

"The one in the yellow trunks," Dave said.

"That one." Cecil nodded miserably. Slowly, painfully, he sat straight, drew in a shaky breath, tenderly clasped his crotch. His white jeans were dirty from the fall he'd taken. He rocked forward and backward, hoping to ease the ache. "I got back from seeing Neil O'Neil just in time to find this kid fooling with the mailbox out by the road. I yelled at him, he ran in here, and I followed him. I wanted to catch him for you. A mistake. A bad mistake." Now he bent with a whimper of pain, and from under the bench picked up Dave's wallet, and handed it to him.

"He brought it back?" Dave opened it. The cash was gone. But the credit cards were all in place. Driver's license, Medicare card, gun permit, everything. A slip of paper fluttered to the bricks. He picked it up. The handwriting was bad, the ballpoint pen was nearly dry of ink, but by squinting he could read it. *The lady with the little kid you was asking about she bought a ticket to Winter Creek.* Dave laughed.

"What's funny?" Cecil said.

"A day late." Dave helped Cecil up off the bench, and supporting him along, helped him cross the humpy, leaf-strewn bricks to the cookshack. "And five hundred dollars short." He opened the screen, unlocked the solid door. "He hangs around that bus station. I guess he sees everything that goes on there." Dave eased Cecil down on a chair at the table, went to the counter, where twenty bottles gleamed, and poured him a stiff brandy. "He knew where Jemmie went, but instead of telling me, he stole my wallet. Now he returns it, and doesn't forget to give me the information I wanted. When I've chased all over the map to find it for myself." He set the blister glass in front of Cecil, who sat with his face on his arms on the deal table. "Drink that." He probed a cupboard. "Here's codeine left over from that last bout I had with the dentist." He popped the cover of the little amber container, shook a fat white pill into Cecil's mutely outstretched hand. "Together, they should kill the pain."

"It's so humiliating." Cecil pushed himself upright, washed the pill down with a swallow of brandy. "I'm tall and I'm fast, and he made a fool out of me."

"It's a question of mental patterns," Dave said, and stroked Cecil's beautiful skull. "The rules he lives by are different from yours. Fairness doesn't figure in them."

Cecil smiled feebly. "Go for the jugular, right?"

"Something like that," Dave said. "I'm sorry it happened to you." He bent and kissed the younger man's mouth, then pulled out another chair and sat at the table. "You going to be all right?"

"I don't know anybody ever died from it," Cecil said. "Happened to me a few times when I was a kid in Detroit. Wondered if I'd ever grow up. But I did."

"Fully," Dave said with a grin.

"Yeah." Cecil winced. "Oh, don't make me laugh."

"Drink your brandy." Dave reached for the instrument on the end of the yellow cupboard. "I have to talk to the police in Winter Creek."

It didn't help. He reported to an adenoidal deputy named Underbridge that Jemmie Engstrom was probably there, that the man she'd been living with in Los Angeles was freshly murdered, that Jemmie with Mike appeared to be running for her life, and that her armed and probably dangerous husband, Dallas, was on his way down there after her, and that they should locate her and see that she was protected. Five minutes of glossolalia would have got through just as well to Deputy Underbridge. He didn't know who any of these people were, he didn't know who Dave was, and if there was a murder in Los Angeles, wasn't that the responsibility of the Los Angeles police, and if they wanted the help of the Winter Creek sheriff's department, then they better phone for it, hadn't they? Click.

Dave groaned disgust, and hung up the yellow receiver. "It's no use. I'm sorry. I wanted to stay with you." He pushed the chair back. "But there's nothing else for it—I've got to go to Winter Creek." He rose and started out of the cookshack. "Are you sure you don't want me to drop you at a hospital?"

"No. I'm feeling better already." Cecil threw Dave his best smile this time, but he still got up off the chair as if he hurt. "I'll lie down till it's time to go to work." He read the worry in Dave's face. "No, really. The brandy and the codeine are working. I'm turning numb. Don't worry, I'll be fine, time you see me next."

When Dave came down from the sleeping loft wearing a blue gingham shirt, Levis, the Sig Sauer in its Bianchi shoulder holster under his leather jacket, Cecil was stretched out full length on the corduroy couch. Dave bent over him. "I'll phone you as soon as I can."

Cecil's hand came up and tapped the bulge the gun made. "You remembered your gun. That is scary."

"If Charlie Pratt still has his shotgun, maybe I won't need it. But Dallas Engstrom owns a lot of firepower."

"You better take me with you." Cecil made a move.

Dave shook his head. "You don't own any cowboy boots. Anyway, you've got editing to do, remember? On your piece about the hostel for runaway teens. It airs tonight—right?"

"I'll phone in sick," Cecil said.

"Forget it. I'm not taking you with me. Look what happens to you when you try to help me." Dave turned away. "I'll be all right." He was almost at the door when he remembered and stopped. "What did you get out of O'Neil?"

"Ho-ho-ho." Cecil tried to sit up, and fell back with a suppressed moan. "You'll love it. I waited out in front of the house in my van, across the street, till he came out. It was so early, and you know how shadowy it is there, I couldn't really see too well—but he came up the steps, opened the trunk, and he's got his arms full, and he drops whatever it is into the trunk. Well, I call to him, jump out, run over with the attaché case. He looks at me, I say my name, and that I'm your associate, and he left his case last night, and here it is, and he's so surprised—he'd figured to come past here to get it, right?—so surprised that he forgets to close the trunk. And guess what's in there. The camouflage suit and boots and helmet."

Dave went back to the couch. "Interesting."

"Isn't it?" Cecil's arm lay across his eyes but he smiled a smug little smile. "And I said, 'Hey, do you play paintball too? What was it—did Vaughn get you into it when you worked together, or what?' And he stammered and stuttered around and finally said that yes, that was it, but he'd only gone once. It wasn't his kind of thing. He prefers tennis and squash."

"Where did Vaughn take him—to the Combat Zone?"

"He 'guesses' that's the name of the place, yes."

"Sunday morning?" Dave held up a hand. "Never mind. Don't tell me. He was much too busy with Sylvia winding up the Shopwise promotion—right?"

Cecil nodded groggily, and mumbled, "Mush too busy."

"I'll call you," Dave said, and left.

Winter Creek lay among rolling hills, fifty miles inland from the Pacific, the San Gregornio mountains hulking to the northeast. It was a quiet place, mostly avocado ranches. But avocados, even with all the improvements in shipping that had come with the years, were still a chancy crop, and a lot of the growers had given up harvesting them long ago. The prices they could get weren't worth the effort. Where they could, Dave saw, they'd sold off the land. But not yet for tract development. As Engstrom had said, people with money were settling here, so the new, rail-fenced ranch houses sprawled on broad acres. Horses browsed the hills. A buckskin yearling, still coltish in the legs, raced along a fence, mane and tail flying, keeping pace for a moment with the Jaguar on the road.

On the outskirts of town, the sheriff had a new sand-color building and a tall flagpole on a neat little grassy five acres that used to be a field with goats and burros and a tumbledown shed. McDonald's had set up yellow arches, a tarmac parking lot, and a glass-and-stone shop on a corner where Dave remembered a sheet-metal gas station. Many more small frame houses looked through aluminum-framed windows at the streets that angled off Main, but Main Street itself was little changed from his last time here. Nothing but the signs on the hardware, barber, and dress shops were new. W. T. Grant's was gone, but K mart had taken its place. Two old men in straw hats sat on kitchen chairs beside the door of the grocery store. A show card taped to the window of the drugstore read VIDEO RENTALS. The movie theater was boarded up. A little more stucco had scaled off the Elks Hall. The tavern, the New Corral, had added cedar planks to its front. A banner across these, UNDER NEW MANAGEMENT, faded in the sun, but the door of the place was in no better repair than when it was just the Corral. Someone had put a boot through it.

And here was the Twin Oaks Café, with a sagging, red, composition roof and faded red trim to its windows, crouching under the big trees that gave it its name. Pickup trucks stood on a rutted parking space beside the café. Dallas Engstrom's wasn't among them. Dave had been keeping an eye out for it as he drove into town. He parked, put on his Stetson, pulled open a squeaky hinged screen door, and walked into smells of chili and barbecue sauce. The counter stools were creaky. Not many were occupied, none of the booths. It was well after lunchtime. The half-dozen drivers of the pickup trucks outside—Levis, work boots, T-shirts washed so often they'd lost their mottos, logos, advertising slogans—lean, leathery men, potbellied men, boys just out of their teens, stuffed with barbecued ribs, chicken-fried steaks, hamburgers, lingered over coffee and filled the air with talk and cigarette smoke.

Hides of coyotes, raccoons, the skin of a rattlesnake were nailed to the Twin Oaks' simulated wood paneling, and over the swing door to the kitchen—faded red again, like the counter top, the tabletops, the cracked false leather of the seats—was mounted a puma's head, tawny fur moth-eaten, mouth open in a dusty snarl, yellow glass eyes dulled by kitchen grease. Under this stood three women in waitress garb, red with white trim, smoking, sipping diet sodas, laughing together, the toughest parts of their day, breakfast and lunch, done with. But they'd noticed Dave the minute he stepped in, and now one of them lounged over. She was forty, growing dumpy, had dyed her hair black, and wore it slicked back to a heavy bun at the nape of her plump neck. A red plastic rose was stuck over her ear. Unlikely as it seemed, somewhere in Winter Creek she'd found a lipstick to match it. The tube wasn't going to last long. She laid it on thick. The name tag on her starchy blouse read CLARICE. She raised amiable, drawn-on eyebrows at him.

"Beck's?" he said with faint hope.

"Dear God," she said. "Where do you think you are, honey, on board of the Concorde?" She patted his hand that lay on the counter. "We got three kinds of beer—West's, and West's light, and West's the expensive one." She glanced along the counter in mock fear. "You want to keep your voice down when you talk about any other brand in Winter Creek. Them West brothers—they got spies everywhere. Word was to get out anybody here even heard of any other beer, their life wouldn't be worth a plug nickel."

No wonder film producers came to Winter Creek. The natives had already memorized the dialogue. "The expensive one," Dave said, and when she brought it back with a glass that featured the West name and dishwasher spots, "thank you." With a pro forma, "You're welcome," she started back to the klatch under the puma's head, and Dave said, "Wait—do you happen to know Dallas Engstrom?"

She swung around, startled. "Yes, but he doesn't live here now—been gone for months."

"He's coming back." Dave poured his beer. "If he isn't here already, he will be soon."

She glanced at a telephone that sat beside the cash register at the end of the counter, then frowned at Dave. "But if he comes back here, the sheriff will lock him up. He's got a warrant out for him. Assault. He knows that."

"He wants his wife and little boy," Dave said.

"They left too, same time he did. Jemmie Pratt," she said. "What a silly fool that girl was. Marrying Dallas Engstrom. He's no better than an animal." She edged off, eyeing the phone again. "I better make a phone call."

"Jemmie came back on Sunday. You haven't seen her?"

"No." Clarice shook her head. So hard the rose fell off her ear. She caught it and put it back with trembling fingers. "No, nobody's mentioned her in here. Listen, just excuse me a minute, okay?"

"Is it Barney Craig you're going to phone?"

"Dallas nearly killed him that night," she said, "beat him up so bad, he was in the hospital for a month. Now, Barney's no angel, either, but him and Dallas—" She broke off and blinked at Dave. She came back to him, leaned close, peering. "Who are you? How do you know so much?"

"Dallas told me all about it. This morning, in L.A. He thought Barney was sleeping with Jemmie," Dave said. "It was a mistake. He knows that now. Barney's in no danger. But Jemmie may be. I have to find her."

"Why?" Clarice was leery now. She straightened, took a step backward. "Who are you? You're not a cop—I've handed out free doughnuts and coffee to cops all my life, and I know a cop when I see one."

"I'm a death claims investigator for insurance companies. My name is Brandstetter." He laid the open license folder on the counter, pushed it toward her between the sugar jar and a bowl of salsa.

She squinted at it a moment, then eyed him warily. "Death claims? That means somebody died and you have to pay, right? Who died, Mr. Death Claims?"

"A boy called Vaughn Thomas." Dave put the folder away. "Last Sunday morning. Somebody shot him with a high-powered rifle." Dave took a sip of beer and looked at her over the glass. "He lived down here for a while—did you know him?"

"The Majorette?" She snorted a brief scornful laugh. She called out to the other waitresses, "Guess what? Somebody shot Vaughn Thomas."

The youngest waitress, all baroque blond hair and high school puppy fat, said, "What with—a paper clip and a rubber band?" Horse-faced, the third waitress showed long teeth and nickered.

Dave stood, laid money on the counter. "How do I get to Charlie Pratt's place?"

Clarice gave him directions.

◆

Pratt was a leathery little man with a stiff left arm and a bad limp. His ranch was rolling pasture land with handsome rail fences. The house was board-and-batten, painted red. The stables looked and smelled clean. Hired hands groomed the big paint horses in the box stalls, exercised them on a long oval track, held lunge straps while they trained colts in paddocks. Out on the meadows other horses grazed. Dave could see this out the windows of Pratt's comfortable office in the house. Trophies, plaques, photographs of a younger Charlie Pratt stood on shelves, hung on the varnished pine plank walls. A bronze racehorse stood on the desk. Pratt stared at Dave over it.

"No, she's not here. Running for her life?" He slapped the desk top. "I knew it. Death is what they live for, that lot." Sometime long ago Pratt had passed time in England. It was still in his speech, just a trace. "Hatred, violence, bloodshed. I tried to warn Jemmie." He blinked. "You got children of your own, Brandstetter?"

"Afraid not," Dave said.

"Then you don't know how girls get. You can't tell them anything. Suddenly, they're eighteen, and they know it all. I was just an old meanie, telling her to keep away from Dallas Engstrom and all his kind."

"I know the story," Dave said. "Dallas told me."

Pratt laughed sourly. "He didn't tell you I was right, did he? Probably told you I was a communist."

Dave grinned. "I doubted it. Not in Winter Creek."

"If you mention the Bill of Rights down here," Pratt said, "you're a communist. If I could, I'd leave, but I can't face moving. Too old, too crippled up." He swiveled his chair and gazed out the window for a moment at the horses on the hills, the mountains in the background, the cloudless sky. "Anyway, it's beautiful. I love it. Besides, I'll be dead soon. And Jemmie—what does she care?"

"Where would she go, since she didn't come here?"

"Why did she come back at all?" Pratt countered.

"I don't know that she did," Dave said, "but if she did, it's to hide from Vaughn's killer."

Pratt smiled bitterly. "She sure can pick 'em, can't she? Think she didn't have good sense. Engstrom was bad enough"—he got to his feet, wincing—"but that Thomas kid—he was certifiable, from what I hear. Deranged. Lucky, I expect, he was killed before he could harm my grandson. Where? I don't know. Engstrom's partner, Craig, I suppose." He limped to the door. "Excuse me, but I've got a sore-footed mare to see to."

Dave stood up. "Where does Craig live?"

Pratt went out the door. His boots knocked the red painted planks of the porch. His voice drifted back, bleak, indifferent. "Try Persimmon Street."

7

◆

The Craig house was one-story pink-cinder-block set on a fifty-by-hundred-fifty-foot lot behind apricot trees. Plump, golden fruit bent the branches, lay splitting open in brown grass. A four-foot-high wire web fence framed the yard. A pickup truck and a stake truck and some kind of yellow-painted earth-moving machine stood on the driveway beside the house. When Dave got there, two sheriff's patrol cars were parked at angles in the street, doors open, top lights turning, staticky voices coming from their two-way radios. Dave parked the Jaguar in roadside weeds across the street, got out, stood watching.

Inside the house, whose door was also open, a man was shouting. Raving might be more accurate. Certainly cursing. And in a minute he came in sight in the doorway, a square-built, balding man of forty, handcuffed behind his back, struggling in the grip of two young, uniformed sheriff's officers whose eyes looked scared, though they kept their pale faces expressionless. They got him down the steps of the poured cement stoop and steered him, lurching and straining, down the walk to the open gate.

"It wasn't me, you donkeys," he said, "it wasn't me."

A goose-necked, slope-shouldered man of sixty followed. He was in uniform too. The uniforms were tan. Those on the two boys were sharply pressed, and maybe this man's had started the day that way, but it was wrinkled, rumpled, crushed now. Even the brown necktie. The two deputies wrestled their stocky captive out the gate, across the width of weeds where a sidewalk might have been if Winter Creek had sidewalks, and into a patrol car. The doors slammed. The two youngsters drove off with the man still raving inside. "If I done it, why didn't I run?"

The goose-necked man turned back toward the house, then heard a siren and stopped to wait until a long black car with the Fortuna County seal on its door pulled up. Not a car, a hearse. The siren moaned into silence. A reedy man in a cowboy hat climbed out of the car, said something to the sheriff, reached back inside for a black leather case, and carrying this walked beside the uniformed man up the path and into the house. Dave crossed the street, followed them, stopped in the open doorway.

The boxy living room was dim because the metal venetian blinds at the windows were closed. But Dave made out a big Nazi flag on one wall, Bavarian beer steins on the mantel under a rack of rifles, a glass case of military decorations on another wall—German, no doubt. And on the pale vinyl tile floor a small young woman lying very still in a position no one would choose to sleep in, legs and arms all wrong. She had been shot. Bullet holes crossed her breast, belly, thighs. There was not a lot of blood. She had died right away. Running and hiding had been no use. He turned away and looked at the untroubled blue sky above the TV-antennaed rooftops of the scruffy little houses. He breathed deeply a few times. Then he swung to the doorway again.

"I was afraid this would happen," he said, and the doctor who was kneeling on the floor by the body lifted his head, and the sheriff, standing against the background of the swastika turned. Dave said, "I telephoned your office at noon, sheriff. From Los Angeles. I suggested to your man Underbridge that he find her and guard her because she was in danger. He wouldn't listen."

The sheriff came to the door. "I'm Claude Rose. Who the hell are you?"

Dave gave his name and showed his license. "Didn't Underbridge tell you about my call?"

"He may have logged it," Rose said. "I didn't look. What do you know about this?"

"That Vaughn Thomas, the man she was living with in Los Angeles, was shot and killed Sunday morning, and that as soon as she learned about it, she took her little boy and ran." He peered at the dimness, felt alarm, and stepped into the room. "Where is he? Mike. Her son. Where is he? Did you send him off earlier?"

"We never saw him," Rose said. "Are you sure—?"

And Dave pushed past him, stepping first into a hallway, banging open a bedroom door, calling, "Mike? Mike? Where are you? It's okay, now. It's over." He knelt and looked under the rumpled bed—dust, beer cans, girlie magazines. He slid open a closet, groped inside. "Mike? You can come out now. The sheriff's here. Everything's under control." No one was in the closet. When he turned to leave, Rose blocked the bedroom doorway.

"How come it's you and not the LAPD?" he said.

"The LAPD decided Thomas's death was a hunting accident. They didn't even know of this girl's existence. I learned about it from someone at his workplace and went to see her. Too late. Plainly she didn't think it was an accident. She knew who killed him, or she knew why he was killed, and she ran off to hide. Nobody knew where. As soon as I knew for sure, I called Underbridge. And when he didn't react, I drove down here. Too late again." Dave pushed the goose-necked man aside. "Look, this can wait. We've got to find that boy. And pray he's still alive."

"What did she come here for?" Rose said.

"This was her home before she ran off with Thomas."

"You mean this house?" Rose waved an arm. "You mean her and Barney Craig—"

"No, I mean she grew up in Winter Creek. She married here. Dallas Engstrom. Surely you've heard of Dallas Engstrom. Famous for busting up barrooms. A big, mean bastard with fists like hammers, and a truckload of guns?"

The sheriff nodded. "That's how I come to know Barney. Engstrom beat hell out of him here last spring. Just before I got transferred here. There's a warrant out for Engstrom."

"Well, now you can use it," Dave said. "He was angry at Jemmie for leaving him and taking Mike. And as soon as he heard from me she'd left Los Angeles, he headed down here."

"What?" Rose scowled. "Then maybe Barney's telling the truth, maybe it wasn't him that killed her. Claimed he walked in and found her dead there on the floor. Called us right away. Says, would he call us and wait for us, if he done it? But we walk in, the fool is standing here staring down at her, with his own M-16 in his hand, just been fired, clip half empty. What would you think?"

"I'd want to know if he killed Vaughn Thomas. Was he up in L.A. Sunday morning? If not, why kill Jemmie? And why wait two days to do it? But we're wasting time." Dave turned away. "We have to find that little boy."

"You sure he's here?" Rose said. "My men went—"

"You take the other bedroom. I'll check the kitchen."

He didn't have to. Hell—Rose's deputies hadn't even been back here. No way could they have missed the bloody little footprints that led Dave onto a screened back porch. Empty beer bottles in their dusty cardboard six-packs were stacked chest high. Dirty laundry, mostly khaki color, lay on a washer-drier pair. Through the screens, in the long backyard, under the corrugated iron roofs of open sheds, Dave glimpsed stacked lumber, bags of cement, cinder blocks, bundles of steel reinforcement rods, a cement mixer.

"Mike?"

The footsteps wobbled to a tall wooden storage cabinet. The doors were smeared with blood where little hands had pawed them. He yanked open the doors. The boy lay huddled, very pale, eyes closed, T-shirt and blue jeans soaked with blood, among cartons and crates. New and unopened. Dave crouched and touched him. Still warm. He bent close. Still breathing. Peanut butter and grape jelly on his breath. Not touching the small body, Dave searched with his eyes for wounds. He saw only a long slice in the scalp under the matted fair hair. Scalp wounds always bled badly. He called, "I found him, sheriff. Bring the doctor."

He got to his feet and distractedly stared at the boxes in the cupboard. Rifle ammunition. Hand grenades. Mortar shells. Even a few guns, CHINA stenciled on the crates that smelled of pine. On the shipping labels was a name and street number in Los Angeles— World Militaria, Inc. No one was coming. He bent and reached for the child, remembered he mustn't be moved, and stepped impatiently into the kitchen. "Doctor!" he shouted.

"I'd like to sell and get out of here," Fern Casper said. She was frail, seventy, dressed in faded jeans, tennis shoes, and a red sweatshirt. Her hair was cropped short. Not artfully—serviceably, probably by herself, with hedge clippers. She had let Dave into her shabby kitchen, and they sat drinking tea at a sticky table where the plates and utensils from many meals were stacked. Also half a dozen dried-out Dinty Moore beef stew cans. A large white hen stalked around the grimy linoleum, clucking to herself. Her sister rested on top of the refrigerator. Fern Casper pulled the dripping bag out of her tea and laid it in a stained saucer. "Something like this was bound to happen. I seen it coming when George Hetzel started training boys in his woods. Them uniforms started appearing in the streets, in the stores. Now they even carry their guns, bold as brass. There was one used to drive around town in a buzzy little red roadster, shooting his gun off in the air." She shook her head. "That's when I put up a 'For Sale' sign."

"I don't blame you." Dave tasted the tea and by reflex reached into the leather jacket. "May I smoke?"

"Nope." She grinned, not quite but almost toothlessly. "Not unless you give me one."

Dave held out the pack. "Are you sure you're eighteen?"

"I'll take a couple of these while I've got the chance," she said, and took six. When he lit the first of them for her, she inhaled deeply, leaned back in the straight kitchen chair, and closed her eyes in contentment. "Ah," she said. Then she let the smoke out and looked at him again. "I don't buy 'em anymore—they slapped a twenty-five-cent tax on last year, you know, and I'm trying to live on Social Security." She sucked greedily on the Marlboro again.

"Why, when I was a girl, they was only fifteen cents for the whole pack, taxes included."

"I remember," Dave said.

"I never stopped smoking," she said. "And I never will. I just have to go a longer time between puffs, is all." Her gnarled fingers touched the white tubes on the table, lining them up neatly. "I appreciate these."

"There are laws against carrying firearms," Dave said. "And laws against shooting them in the streets."

"Laws!" she scoffed. "Sheriff here before, that died, Ron Lutz—he was close with Hetzel as two peas in a pod. And this new one, Rose—he's scared to death of the man."

"He's not alone, is he?" Dave said. "None of your neighbors will talk to me."

"Barney Craig is high up in Hetzel's outfit," she said, "and yes, they're scared of Hetzel. So are most folks in Winter Creek. Only one I heard of that isn't—he's a black man, and he ought to be. Alexander's his name, professor, or something. They burned a cross in his front yard. Killed his dog. Hounded his children out of school. But he won't budge." She smoked her cigarette for a silent moment, drank some tea, set down the cup. "Some others pretend to laugh Hetzel off and call him a nut case—which, of course, he is. But there's fear under the laughter. And when somebody dies and it connects to Hetzel, not many in Winter Creek are likely to answer questions about it, yours or the sheriff's either. They're afraid they'll get shot too."

"Not you," Dave said.

She said, "That's 'cause I haven't got any answers."

"You didn't see who went in there this afternoon?"

She shook her head. "I heard the shots, that was all."

"Barney Craig claims he came in a few minutes later, found her dead, killed with one of his rifles."

"Maybe. I didn't see him. Truth is, I'm mostly back here. Since my television broke down, I don't go in the front room hardly at all. My bedroom's just across the hall from here, bathroom beside it. So I don't know what goes on on the street out front unless it makes a loud noise. And if it makes a loud noise—like them shots—I figure it's smarter to stay where I am, out of sight."

"You didn't know that Jemmie, the dead girl, was living there?" Dave said. "You didn't see or hear the little boy?"

"Barney Craig's been part of Hetzel's outfit for years now," she said, and gently tapped ashes off her cigarette into a greasy soup bowl. "He's my neighbor, so if we chance to meet, of course I say hello—but I steer clear of him if I can, and when I have to go out front to get the mail or put out the trash, I don't even look his way. I mind my own business, and hope he'll mind his."

"His partner," Dave said. "Dallas Engstrom?"

"The tall one with the long, yellow hair." She nodded. "Worse than Craig by a country mile. Barney's a worry with all them guns. But Engstrom—he was deadly just with his fists. And I think Vietnam did something to his mind. It did to a lot of boys, you know—I seen that on the TV. They just never get right in their heads again, some of them. Sad." She thought about this glumly for a moment, then went on. "You know, Dallas turned on Barney—best friends they was, I used to see them over there, laughing together, never a cross word between them—and he near beat him to death, here, not too long ago." She gave a shaky laugh. "Wouldn't be likely to beat up a little old lady, I guess, but all the same, I breathed easier when I heard he left town."

"He's back in town," Dave said. "It's possible he was the one who murdered Jemmie. They were married, you know."

"I guess I knew that once," Fern Casper said. "I forget things lately. Pratt girl, wasn't she, just out of high school? Ran off to Las Vegas?"

"And six years later," Dave said, "the same night her husband beat up Barney Craig and threatened to beat her too, she ran off with another man."

"Mmm-hmm." The old woman nodded but had she heard? Pinching the tip of the cigarette between long, dirty nails, she pulled the last smoke out of the butt, then regretfully snubbed the little coal out in the soup bowl. She looked at Dave for a moment as if she didn't know how he came to be there. Then her eyes cleared and she said, "I wouldn't want him to be jealous of me. Not Dallas Engstrom."

Dave stood up, pushing back his chair and startling the hen who'd come to rest under it. She squawked and flapped away. The one on the refrigerator stood up for a minute, surprised, then settled down again. Dave said, "If you see him, telephone the sheriff, will you?"

"No," she said, with that impish three-fanged smile. "Haven't got a phone." She stood up, nowhere near as tall as his shoulder, and touched him with a grubby hand. "Just a joke. I'll run next door to the Huffstatlers."

"Thank you." Dave pushed open the screen door. The big white hen ran out between his legs. "Even if they wouldn't talk to me, maybe the neighbors will talk to you. See what you can learn, and I'll come back tomorrow, if I may?"

"You better—I'll be out of smokes by then."

He bought a carton of cigarettes in the drugstore, a place as shiny with glass and chrome and cold fluorescent lighting as if it were in L.A.—Johnny Walker, a pack of throw-away razors, a can of shave cream, toothbrush, tooth powder, a stick of deodorant, a pack of T-shirts, a pack of shorts, two pairs of half wool, half nylon socks. In the toy department he plucked from a rack of green wire a couple of plastic-bubbled cardboards, one holding a Transformer tank, the other a Transformer cement mixer truck. In another part of the store, he negotiated a bigger purchase, but that he left behind for the manager to dispose of.

He took the rest in a white plastic sack to a motel called the Ranchero, built of cement bricks with lots of runny mortar, all painted very white under a red roof whose tiles were not tiles. The metal boxes of air-conditioning units stuck out of every window and dripped on the long cement walkways. He bought a bag of ice cubes from a machine in an alcove. He showered, put on the new underwear, took the sanitary wrap off a plastic glass and dropped ice cubes into the glass and poured whiskey over them. Then he sat down on a bed under a framed print of Charlie Russell cowboys branding calves, lit a cigarette, stretched out, and phoned the TV station in L.A.

"How are you feeling?" he said.

"It's gone away," Cecil said. "I'm okay now. Thanks. How are things down there?"

Dave told him how things were.

"Maybe Mike saw who it was," Cecil said.

"I hope so," Dave said. "Because if any of the neighbors did, they're not saying."

"You think it was Engstrom?"

"He lied to me about where he was the morning Vaughn Thomas was killed," Dave said, "but that doesn't have to mean he killed him. And if he didn't, if he wasn't afraid Jemmie could implicate him, why would he kill Jemmie?"

Cecil said, "Could finding her living with Barney drive him to it?"

"Maybe. He's got a short fuse," Dave said, "but beating your buddy and your wife is one thing—murder's another. I don't know—it doesn't feel right to me. And nobody's seen Engstrom here. If he showed, somebody should have noticed. He's conspicuous, and everybody's afraid of him." Dave sighed, took a drag from his cigarette. "I'll be going to the hospital later to talk to Mike. They expect him to come to by evening. He's in shock, lost a lot of blood, and the bullet gave him a concussion. He's only five years old. He may not remember anything." Dave raised himself on an elbow and took a drink of the whiskey. Johnny Walker Red had been his father's brand. He hadn't tasted it in years. It brought back memories of days long lost, good days, when he was young, younger anyway, and when a lot of people he cared about were still alive who were alive no longer. Max Romano for one. Damn. Memories were ambushing him too often these days. *A foolish, fond old man.* He drew a deep, steadying breath and said to Cecil, "What's happening at your end?"

"The police have changed their minds about Kaminsky. Now they're saying he didn't fall, after all."

"I never thought he did," Dave said.

"You thought somebody pushed him, right?"

Dave blinked at the receiver. "And the police don't?"

"There was tar on the soles of his shoes. He went up to the roof, Dave. It's a flat roof, and it was resurfaced recently. He walked across it, then he stood on the raised edge, on the tiles. His shoe prints are plain, there. He jumped, Dave."

"Somebody had a gun in his back," Dave said.

"There was only one set of footprints in the tar. Dave—Kaminsky committed suicide."

When Dave walked into the Twin Oaks Café at sunset, news was yapping from a radio back of the counter. Clarice called, "Mr. Death Claims?" and pointed to a booth in a corner. "Sit there, so's I can wait on you." He sat in the booth and laid the Stetson beside him on the cracked red plastic seat pad. The sun shone in his eyes. She came, set down a jingling glass of ice water for him, leaned across, and tugged a cord that lowered a rattling bamboo blind. "You was right," she said. "Dallas come and killed his wife, like you said, and now"—her voice wobbled, a tear ran down her face, she wrung her hands—"Barney's in jail for it."

"You've seen Dallas, someone told you they saw him?"

She shook her head, took a paper napkin from the square shiny dispenser on Dave's table, and blew her nose, and dried her tears. "But it had to be him, didn't it? Crazy murdering son of a bitch. Why'd she have to come back here, anyways, and bring him tagging after her?"

"That part I'm sure she didn't plan," Dave said.

Clarice laughed a shaky vengeful laugh. "Well, she's damn sorry now, if she did or if she didn't."

"So am I." Dave reached for a red plastic folder that held a menu card behind yellowed plastic. He took reading glasses from his jacket, put them on, peered at the handwritten list. "What's to eat?"

"You're a cool one, aren't you?" she said.

"In my line of work," he said, "it doesn't help to get emotional. It interferes with thinking."

"It was Barney's gun," she said bitterly. "They'll never let him off."

Dave peered up at her over the glasses. "I thought you and Barney had split up."

"Oh, we had some silly argument," she said. "I can't even remember what it was about, now. TV or baseball or something. But then Dallas near killed him, and he landed up in the hospital. And the way I felt when I heard—well it come to me he was the only man I cared about in the world. And I run over there and told him I loved him, and I'd stick by him, and he mustn't die. And that was it. We been seeing each other regular ever since."

"Dallas didn't know that." Dave folded and put away the glasses. "His old jealousy of Barney must have flared up again today, when he found Jemmie hiding there."

"That poor, dumb girl might still be alive," she said, "if you'd have let me phone Barney and warn him."

"She wouldn't have answered, and he wasn't at home," Dave said. "He was out on a job site. Waiting for laborers who never showed up. So he told the sheriff."

She stared. "You mean that's his alibi?"

"Off in the hills. Nobody saw him." Dave set the menu back in its place. "The barbecued ribs, please."

Writing it down, she looked glum. But professional cheerfulness chirped in her voice. "I'll bring a hot towel with them for your fingers, sir. We're world famous for our ribs." She breezed off. "You won't be sorry."

He was sorry, but not surprised.

8

◆

On the edge of town, the hospital and its parking lot took up maybe two acres of what had once been an avocado grove. The building was a new one of pale brick, with glass doors, aluminum-framed windows, a roof of brown fake tile, fireproof, rainproof, windproof. The plan was simple. The building surrounded a patio. He could see the tops of four avocado trees above the roof line.

He left the Jaguar on the tarmac in a slot marked VISITORS and pushed into a lighted reception area where the temperate air smelled of disinfectant and vitamin B. The nurse at the reception desk had her back to glass sliding doors that opened onto the patio, where light escaping from hospital rooms showed flower beds and wooden seats under the trees. Maybe patients sat out there sometimes. The patio was tiled in terra-cotta squares, and it looked a pleasant place, as places in hospitals went.

For his part, he'd had his fill of hospitals. It was another good reason he'd retired. Home safe in the canyon reading books and listening to music and sometimes hauling his little typewriter out of a deep desk drawer and trying to write about his cases—doing these harmless things, minding his own affairs instead of those of resentful strangers, he wasn't so apt to be shot, stabbed, drowned, burned up, car-wrecked as he'd been when he worked. He laughed grimly to himself. So what was he doing here?

The nurse was plump, gray-haired, wore no makeup, and probably sang in a church choir. When he told her it was little Mike Engstrom he'd come to see, she smiled sentimentally and explained to him, with gestures, how to find the room. Her smile faded. "Poor little thing. Mother shot to death right in front of his eyes." She clucked. "How is he going to get over that? A person would never forget a thing like that. Not their whole life long."

"He remembers, then?" Dave said.

"Not yet. He hasn't woken up yet."

Dave went to the room anyway. A sheriff's deputy sat on a brown molded plastic chair with spindly black iron legs outside the room door. He was one of the boy children who had escorted Barney Craig out of his house this afternoon, scared even though the man was in handcuffs. A tattered *Reader's Digest* was in the deputy's hands. He looked up at Dave. Without recognition. Dave showed him his license, and told him:

"I'm hoping he can describe the one who shot her."

"So's Sheriff Rose," the boy said. "He's having his supper." He looked at his watch. "Be here soon." He held out his hand for Dave to shake, and said, "I'm Bob Lowry." Rubber soles squeaked on the clean hallway floor, and a balding young man in white stepped around them and pushed into the room. Dave got a glimpse of the small boy in the big bed. A nurse got up off a chair beside the bed, above which hung a bottle. A tube from the bottle connected to Mike's arm. What were they piping into him? Whatever it was, Dave hoped it would wake him. The door clicked shut. Dave sat on a chair like the deputy's, across from him, against the other wall, beside a window on whose sill other ragged magazines were stacked. Lowry said, "Insurance?"

Dave lied. "Vaughn Thomas's—the man Jemmie was living with in L.A. He was killed in what the police claim was a shooting accident. I think it was murder, and whoever killed him killed her."

"What for?" the deputy asked.

"When we find him," Dave said, "maybe he'll tell us."

"We're looking for her husband"—Lowry's fair, childish forehead wrinkled—"Dallas Armstrong?"

"Engstrom," Dave said. "No luck yet?"

"Not that I heard. Armed and dangerous, Sheriff Rose says. Hell, lots of armed and dangerous around here now. Crazy people." He wrinkled his nose. "You ever seen one of those skinheads?"

"You're talking about George Hetzel's crew? Vaughn Thomas was part of it for a while."

The boy cocked his head. "For a while? What happened? Did Hetzel throw him out?"

"On the contrary," Dave said. "Thomas had a wealthy father, not only wealthy but old. Hetzel was counting on Vaughn for heavy financial help in the future. He made the boy a major in his lunatic brigade. I gather he was free to do anything he liked. And when he up and left in the middle of the night, Hetzel was furious."

"Maybe Hetzel killed him," the deputy said. "I sure as hell wouldn't want him furious at me."

"I thought Hetzel was all mouth," Dave said.

Lowry moved his eyebrows skeptically. "So did I—till that housing project burned down."

Dave sat straight. "The one he'd been talking against on television, got up petitions about, lobbied Sacramento?"

Lowry nodded. "Burned down one night, a few months back. Wasn't finished. They just had the framework up, you know, roof, wiring, plumbing. Big place—you should have seen it. Fire companies from all over. No use. Forty-, fifty-mile-an-hour winds. I never saw anything burn so fast and so hot."

"And you think it was Hetzel's doing?"

Lowry shrugged. "He was the one who tried to turn everybody against it, said welfare drones would be moving in, upping our taxes, and they'd be black, and that meant crime and drugs and gangs. Winter Creek would be ruined."

"Wasn't it federally funded, at least partly?"

"Oh, hell, yes. And the FBI was down on Hetzel like a grasshopper plague. He just smiled and opened his files for them, and they never got a thing on him. But it was a set fire, all right. Started with gasoline on a slope below the project, dry grass and brush. Wind swept the flames up the hill, whoosh. Probably didn't take a minute."

"You said it wasn't finished," Dave said. "No one had moved in yet. So there were no casualties."

"One. Night watchman, security guard. Old man." Lowry whispered a sorry laugh. "Black man, wouldn't you know? He didn't stand a chance. Maybe he was asleep. We found him in his little guard shed. There's insurance on a project like that, isn't there? Sure. It can be rebuilt. But nobody can give Mr. Alexander his life back, can they? Hetzel got himself a bonus. Killed a 'nigger,' right?"

The room door opened. The young doctor leaned out and said to Lowry, "He's awake."

"I have to stand guard here," Lowry said, and touched the big brown .45 revolver in a holster on his hip. "Can you phone the sheriff and tell him?"

"I can't leave him," the doctor said. "We're not sure if he even knows his mother is dead. It's a delicate time. He has to be handled with great care."

Dave stood up. "Tell me the number. I'll phone."

A half hour later, Dave sat on a bench in the patio under the rustling trees and smoked a cigarette. Leaves came down from the trees, blown off by a wind that had nighttime chill to it, surprising after a hot day to anyone not used to these inland valleys that were, after all, almost desert before men had piped in water and made them fruitful. He liked to picture them as they used to be, the scattered oaks casting shadows on the soft, mossy green of the spring hills, the tawny hills of summer, the dry brown hills of winter, lost and empty under the sky, before the coming of roads and towns and orchards, when this chunk of the Pacific Shelf was by geographical, linguistic, religious, and every other logic part of Mexico, and where, those rare times when smoke rose into this high and lonely sky, it came from a mesquite fire built by the women of some scruffy, wandering Indian family, for roasting rabbit or quail, or stewing deer meat with berries to twist into pemmican.

His cigarette burned him. He dropped it hastily and put his fingers to his mouth, and Sheriff Rose stepped onto the patio. He looked glum, came and sat down on the bench next to Dave, pushed back his hat, shook his head, sighed. "It's no use my talking to him," he said.

"He's scared of me. I don't know why he should be, but you can tell, you know? A little kid's face shows everything they're thinking."

"What did you ask him?"

"I went careful—you heard what the doctor said. I just give him a smile and said I was sorry he was hurt, but he seemed like a brave boy to me, and the pain would let up soon and he'd feel fine again. Before he knew it, he'd be up and out of the hospital."

"He didn't ask for his mother?"

Rose glanced at Dave and away. "You'd have thought that would be the first thing. 'My mama's hurt, is she all right?'—something like that. But nope. Not a word. He just glanced at me a second with those blue eyes of his and turned his head away on the pillow. I talked to him awhile longer. Asked him if he liked horses. And did he know his grandpa had a lot of horses. And his grandpa was coming to see him. He looked at me again for a second there. It was plain to see he couldn't make any sense out of that."

"They've never met," Dave said. "Jemmie refused to have anything to do with Charlie Pratt after he tried to keep her from marrying Engstrom."

"Pratt didn't tell me that. I went and told him what had happened to his daughter, you know. That's not the part of sheriffing I like. Mostly in Fortuna County, it's high school kids killed drunk driving Saturday nights on the highway you got to tell their folks about. And it never gets easy, no matter how often it happens—and it happens, I get to thinking, damn near every weekend of the world." He sat forward, elbows on knees, hands dangling. He took off his hat, stared at it, turning it in his fingers. "Beautiful children, smashed to a pulp, their blood all over the road. My God, my God—what's the point of it?"

"What about Pratt?" Dave said.

"He took it hard. Didn't let on—not with words. He went right on measuring oats into tin feed bins he had set out there beside the stable building. A man like that, a jockey, you know, that's a dangerous way to make a living. They can get hurt bad. I suppose they learn early not to show pain. But the news about the girl broke him up inside. I knew it. And I thought I won't ask him to come look at her for a positive ID, you know. Not till tomorrow. But he excused himself to me, went and got a youngster to come finish with the oats, picked up his hat, and says, 'I guess you'll want me to see her, won't you?'

"And I drove him into town, to Cole's Funeral Home—which is where we take the dead bodies here in Winter Creek—and I walked him into the cold room. And she's laying there under a sheet on a table, and he stopped, and I went and turned back the sheet from her face, and he stood staring for a minute, not a flicker in his face, then he nods and says, 'That's her. That's my Jemmie,' and there's kind of a tremble in his voice when he says her name, and he turns away real quick and leaves—got a limp, you know, but he walked fast. I didn't catch up to him till he was outside, climbing in my car. He stared out the window, didn't speak a word on the ride back out to his ranch. Not even goodbye, when I dropped him off." Rose sighed. "Yup. He's hurt bad. Oh"—he stood up and kicked at leaves on the tiles—"I tell you, I hate that part of sheriffing."

Dave stood too. "I'll go talk to Mike."

Gauze and tape swathed his skull. Their whiteness gave his pale skin a touch of color just by contrast. He lay propped on pillows. Distrust was in his eyes, which were Dallas Engstrom's eyes but without the anger. Dave hoped the anger would never come, but that was against common sense, against the way life really went. From the doorway, Dave said, "Hello, Mike. My name is Dave." He dipped into the pockets of the leather jacket and brought out the bright plastic toys and held them up. "I brought these."

The eyes livened up. "Transformers!" the little voice squeaked. "Oh, boy. For me?"

Dave went into the room. "I've been in hospitals a lot myself. And I know there's not much to do." He found a white straight chair and sat down on it. "I thought you might like playing with them."

Mike held out his hands. Kaminsky had been right—they were big hands for a five-year-old. "I love Transformers," he said. Dave gave them to him. He turned them over and over, laughing at his luck. He looked at Dave. "Wow, I never saw these ones before." He laid the tank aside, and began a close, frowning study of the mixed cement truck. "Wow," he whispered to himself.

"I didn't bring the instructions," Dave said, "but I learned how to work them myself, and I can show you. Oh, I almost forgot." He dug out of his pocket two tiny figures, one yellow, one blue. "These go with the truck. They're called Boomer and Ricochet. They're robots, but they turn into guns."

Mike took them. "I know that," he said scornfully. "That's what Transformer means." He fidgeted with the figures. Gun barrels popped out. He examined the truck again, then inserted pegs on the robots into holes on the truck's cement drum. "See? An armored vehicle."

Dave said, "It's a big robot too. Let me show you."

"It's okay," Mike said. "I can do it." He turned the truck's cab inside out, upside down. "There's his feet." He clicked a pair of arms out from under the rear wheels, then popped the robot's head out of the end of the cement mixer barrel. He detached Boomer and Ricochet from the barrel and fastened them in the robot's fists. He lowered and raised the arms. "Zap," he said, "zap." He turned one arm outward from the body. "Zap," again, and the other arm, "zap." He looked at Dave, eyes shining. "They're cool."

"I think so," Dave said. "I never had any before. I almost didn't bring them. I wanted to keep them and play with them myself."

Mike giggled. "Be serious. You're too old."

"No, really." Dave picked up the tank and ran it along the surface of the little bedside table. "Look at that. Fire comes out the back."

"Wow," Mike said, and reached for it.

"It turns into a robot too," Dave said.

"It better, or it's not a Transformer," Mike said, and proceeded to slide the front and back halves of the small brown killer vehicle an inch apart, stand it upright, and raise its stiff arms.

Dave said, "The gun turret turns."

"Oh, hey," Mike said, and turned it left, right. "Pow," he said softly, "pow." Then he laid it down on the wash-faded, very clean coverlet, beside the cement truck, and looked at Dave with his head tilted. "You know what happened to me? A man came in the house and my mother heard him and she went to see who it was and he had a gun and he shot her. Over and over. I told him to stop, and he shot me too."

"Who was the man?" Dave said. "Did you know him?"

"Only I'm not dead," Mike said, as if he hadn't heard. "And she's dead." His eyes searched Dave's. "Isn't she?"

"I'm afraid so," Dave said. "It's not your fault, Mike. You couldn't stop him. You know that. He had the gun."

"I ran and hid," Mike said. "I was afraid he'd shoot me over and over too. When they shoot you over and over, you're a floppy. That's what Dallas says. A floppy."

"Who was the man?"

"I don't know. He had a helmet and a face shield, and I couldn't see."

"Camouflage clothes?" Dave asked.

Mike nodded, picked up the tank, and handed it to Dave. "Run it on the table so I can see the fire again."

Dave did as he was told. He looked at the child watching the buzzing, sparking toy. "It wasn't Barney, was it?"

"No. Barney was good to us." He frowned. "Where's Vaughn?" He looked toward the door through which Dave had come, as if the dead boy might be the next to surprise him with a visit. "Jemmie said he'll come when he can."

"The man with the gun wasn't Vaughn. Was it your dad?"

Mike was scornful again. "Dallas? Dallas is big and tall." He underlined the word with his small voice and beamed at the notion of how tall his father was, taller in his mind, Dave suspected, than anyone. "And Dallas wouldn't kill Jemmie. They loved each other. I'm their little boy. You have to be in love to have a little boy."

"But he hit her sometimes," Dave said, "didn't he?"

"Sometimes," Mike nodded, "but that wasn't him—that was just the beer—that's what Jemmie says." Mike folded the robot into a cement truck again. "Maybe it was a sheriff or a policeman. Maybe it was Mr. Hetzel."

"Was it Mr. Hetzel?" Dave said, surprised.

"Vaughn says they're not our friends. They want to hurt us. He made me say it over and over so I wouldn't forget—'we never tell anything to a sheriff, or a policeman, or Mr. Hetzel.' " He looked at Dave warily. "You're not Mr. Hetzel, are you?"

"No, and I'm not a sheriff or a policeman, either," Dave said. "I'm a friend. And it's important that you tell me who the man was, Mike. I have to find him and have him locked up, so he can't kill anyone else."

Mike looked at the toys on the coverlet, touched them, sighed, and said hopelessly, "I don't know who he was."

The door opened. Weatherbeaten old Charlie Pratt stood there, a very large, very new teddy bear tucked under his stiff left arm. His eyes were red and swollen. He smiled awkwardly and said, "Mike, I'm your grandpa Charlie, your mother's daddy. It's time we got acquainted."

"You're the one with horses," Mike said.

"They wouldn't let me bring a horse in here." The old jockey held out the bear. "This was the best I could do."

9

◆

Dave had expected high chain-link fence with razor wire on top, armed guards at the gates, raving attack dogs. The headlights of the Jaguar showed him nothing like that. Only a modest three-bedroom ranch house set back on a lawn with big old eucalyptus trees, azalea bushes under the windows. Hung to the eaves of the shake roof were lights that pushed back the darkness a little, but they were nothing unusual. He left the Jaguar at the road edge. Surrounded by silence, he made for the house. What was that? He glanced back. A shape ducked quickly out of sight behind the car. Off to his left, a walkie-talkie crackled for a split second. He'd been right about the guards, anyway. He pressed the bell push, and a click made him look up. A camera had its glass eye on him. A voice came from nowhere, thinned by circuitry.

"Yes? Who's there?"

"Dave Brandstetter. Insurance investigator. Looking into the death of Vaughn Thomas. Like to ask you a few questions, if I may?"

Pause. "Go to your left. Take the walk to the back. You'll be met there."

Two males in skivvy shirts and fatigue pants waited outside the door of an add-on room at the rear of the house. Its lighted windows showed Dave office equipment. The guards didn't give him time to stare. They turned him. Roughly. One had a coarse five-day growth of black beard. Twigs and leaves were stuck in his long hair. The other was high school age, clean-shaven, even his scalp. It gleamed. His pretty arms were tattooed and he smelled of Lifebuoy soap. The older one just smelled. "Hands on top of the car." It was a nondescript gray compact, possibly a rental. He did as he was told. Hands slapped his thighs. "Spread 'em." The unwashed one, crouching, ran hands up and down Dave's legs. The skinhead patted his torso. "Jesus, will you look at this." He yanked Dave around to face him. "What did you think you were doing, bringing a gun in here?"

"I didn't want to be different," Dave said.

"Mr. Hetzel." The tattooed boy banged on the door, which was painted with a double lightning bolt. The door opened. A fortyish man looked at Dave through rimless glasses from a bland, oval face. He wore a short-sleeved white shirt, tie, the trousers of a gray business suit. "He come armed, sir," the skinhead said.

"Yes," Hetzel said, and held out a hand. "I'll take it, sergeant, thank you." He turned the Sig Sauer over in his hand, light glowing on its bronze finish. "A fine piece, Brandstetter. Swiss Army regulation." He looked at the skinhead again, and at the bearded one. "That's all, men," he said, "dismissed." The skinhead threw him a salute and a "Sir!" and clicked his heels before leaving. The smelly one just slouched off into the dark, scratching an armpit.

Unsmiling, Hetzel said to Dave, "Come in, Brandstetter. I want to talk to you." He walked away from the door. Dave stepped inside and closed the door. A spring lock clicked. Hetzel threaded his way between file cabinets, typewriters, computers, printers, copying machines, to a desk, where he opened a drawer and dropped the Sig Sauer into it. The room was piled with boxes of office supplies. Worktables were heaped with printed form letters and window envelopes. The place looked like any office devoted to a cause, except for the guns and the Nazi flag beside the Stars and Stripes back of Hetzel's chair. "Sit down. You're older than I thought."

"I've still got my teeth." Dave put himself on a metal folding chair. "Anyway, why the interest in my age? Who am I to you?"

"The traitor who put Colonel Lothrop Zorn, a true patriot and brave marine, in prison. Disgraced him and destroyed an operation built to defend this country against enemies within and without." Hetzel spoke as if by rote. The phrases probably weren't always arranged in this order. But he'd used them a lot. No wonder he hadn't been a winner on television. "The President of the United States had offered a reward to anyone who could capture and deliver for trial, leading to conviction, any terrorist or terrorists who—"

"I remember the case," Dave said. "But you're wrong. I didn't destroy Zorn. Duke Summers did."

"You were behind it," Hetzel said.

"Don't you respect Summers?" Summers was, on a higher and far more secret level, as powerful in U.S. intelligence as half a dozen CIA directors, and had been for decades. No one of Hetzel's political leanings would dream of faulting Duke Summers. Not without knowing what Dave had learned about Summers when they were both twenty-two years old, serving with army intelligence in snowy, shell-shattered Berlin just after World War II. Dave had risked his neck to save Summers's career then. But only the two of them would ever know that. Dave didn't admire that career. But that was another story. He smiled. "Of course you do. Why, Gorbachev would be running this country from Omaha today if it wasn't for Duke Summers."

"I don't like you," Hetzel said in his flat voice. "And I don't put up with people I don't like. I have a mission—to save this country from the Jews and the niggers and the mongrel hordes of South America and Asia, and give it back to the white people. And I don't get a lot of help with that. Whole United States feels the way I do, but they've been brainwashed by the liberal network TV traitors to where they're afraid to speak out plainly. I have to reach those people, and I will, I will. But it takes a lot of time and energy, most of it mine. So tell me what you're doing here, and let's get it over with."

"Vaughn Thomas came down here last spring and enrolled in your guerrilla warfare training program," Dave said. "I don't know what qualifications you expect of your candidates, but I'm told his was a donation of five thousand dollars to your cause. He spent a few months here—three, was it?—and then one night he decamped. Very suddenly. And you were upset about it. Mad as hell, in fact."

Now Hetzel smiled. It wasn't meant for cheerful. It was meant to chill the blood. "I don't get mad, Brandstetter. I get even."

Dave stared. "You know what you're saying?"

"I know better than that," Hetzel said easily. "I know no one is listening. There's only the two of us here, and anything you tell anyone about this meeting of ours will only be your word against mine. I know that Vaughn Thomas was killed by a rifle bullet up in Los Angeles. I saw it on the Monday morning news on television."

"Maybe—but you knew about it before that, right?"

"I never said so," Hetzel said.

"But you were up in L.A. on Sunday?"

"I was not. I was in Columbia, South Carolina, at a white-power conference. I was the keynote speaker."

"You could have sent somebody to L.A. to do the job." Dave tilted his head toward the door. "The one with the insect life in his hair looks as if he'd enjoy it."

"To what point? Why would I want Vaughn Thomas dead? I loved the boy. I felt he had real potential. Uncanny how we thought alike. He could have been my son."

"He was Steven Thomas's son," Dave said. "Thomas is old and has a bad heart. And Vaughn told you that when he died, he, Vaughn, would inherit millions, and he was going to turn all of it over to you for your work. I've seen it before—losing out on millions can make a man angry enough to kill."

"Not this man. It was only a matter of waiting. Vaughn would have come back. He was happy here, said so with tears in his eyes. He'd found his true home." Hetzel's face darkened. "He only left because of that girl. She's the one who sealed his fate."

"You saying she shot him?" Dave said.

"I didn't mean that," Hetzel said, "but if he'd stayed here in Winter Creek, it wouldn't have happened." His eyes behind their shiny lenses narrowed. He pointed a finger. "Dallas Engstrom started it, beating her, sending her into Vaughn's arms. A married woman with a child."

"Little Mike," Dave said. "He told me tonight that Vaughn was afraid of you. He sure as hell was afraid of something. Several people noticed that. Jumped every time the phone rang at his office. He was in hiding. Gave a false address on his job application. Didn't even put a telephone in at his apartment. Why?"

"Afraid of me? Hiding from me?" Hetzel snorted a laugh. "Ridiculous. Little children make things up, you know that."

"Grownups make things up too, Hetzel."

"Use your common sense," Hetzel said. "Did Vaughn leave here alone? Fleeing in fear? He did not. He left with Jemmie Engstrom. She was pretty and helpless and came running to him to save her. Vaughn was only a boy. He had no defenses against a woman like that."

"About Engstrom—he claims you dismissed him a few years back for a barroom brawl. Is that true?"

"Not for a barroom brawl, no. He was uncontrollable, and he put ARAMMO in danger. Some of the trainees in his platoon got hurt—one of them nearly died. Their families threatened to sue. We had to settle out of court to keep the story quiet. It cost a lot of money—and we can't afford that." Hetzel sighed. "He was a fine instructor. He knew how tough it was out there, and he was tough on his boys, and they came out real fighting men. He'd learned from experience. In Vietnam, that war we ran away from, betraying all those boys who'd given the last full—"

"I thought you didn't want to waste time," Dave said.

Hetzel didn't hear. His face had grown red. "The Jew communist scum here at home, the very people I want to stop—marching in the street, burning the flag, making cowards out of Congress—betrayed our brave fighting—"

"You were telling me about Dallas Engstrom," Dave said.

"What?" Hetzel blinked, drew breath, and his blood pressure dropped a little. "Engstrom killed Vaughn. Of course he did. For stealing his wife. Then he killed her. Just this afternoon. Here in

Winter Creek. At Barney Craig's house. Naturally that idiot Rose arrested Barney."

"Craig is your chief lieutenant," Dave said. "Why haven't you bailed him out?"

"Oh, no." Hetzel held up his hands. "A murder scandal could destroy us. The media will try to connect it to the Movement. It's Barney's business, private, personal, nothing to do with us. I can't touch it. My supporters are Christians, old-fashioned, respectable people, not educated, not sophisticated, but they know right from wrong—and they don't want the Movement made to look sordid and squalid. That's not the America I'm fighting to bring back."

"The America where you burn crosses on a neighbor's lawn because he's black?" Dave said. "Kill his dog? Drive his children out of school?"

Hetzel thrust out his jaw. "Blacks have no business in Winter Creek. This is a white community. What did Alexander want to move in here for? To make trouble, that's all."

"I had it backwards," Dave said. "I thought you were the one who made the trouble."

"I had nothing to do with it. I tell you, the people down here have old-fashioned values—and the races don't mix, Brandstetter. I don't care if he calls himself a professor, I don't care if he earns two hundred thousand dollars a year, he's a nigger. And when niggers try to move in on white people, that's the time to draw the line."

"Or set a fire?" Dave said.

Hetzel lost color. For a few seconds his mouth moved without words coming out of it. Then his color returned, and he leaned across the desk, jabbing with that finger. "You listen to me. I had nothing to do with that fire. ARAMMO had nothing to do with it."

"You didn't want that housing complex built," Dave said. "You fought it every inch of the way, talks on television, mailers, petitions, a delegation to Sacramento."

"All legitimate means," Hetzel said. "Constitutional. But people get stirred up over a thing like that. Feelings run deep. But"—he spread his hands—"I can't be held responsible for the violent actions of every deranged nut running loose in Fortuna County."

"You did stir them up, though, right? You admit that?"

"I wanted to stir sane people up," Hetzel said. "Bring them to their senses."

"And when you failed at that, when legitimate measures didn't work, you resorted to illegitimate ones, desperate ones."

"No. Absolutely not. Ask the FBI." Hetzel's arm swung at the row of cabinets. "They got a court order, and went through those files with a fine-tooth comb. Questioned me for hours. Interviewed everybody here. Took 'em days. Four agents. Nothing. They didn't turn up one shred of evidence pointing to me."

"I'm sure they didn't," Dave said.

"You're sneering," Hetzel said. "Well, let me tell you something nobody else knows. They didn't settle for a legitimate search. They broke in here later and searched again. Made it look like some left-wing crowd did it or something. Careless, threw stuff around. But it was them, all right, wasn't it? Trying to catch me off guard, in case I'd hidden something from them before."

"Shocking," Dave said. "It still doesn't mean you didn't send your Bathless Wonder out there"—he jerked his head at the office door—"off over the hills with a match and a can of gasoline that night, does it? That wouldn't require any paperwork."

Hetzel jumped to his feet. "Get out of here."

"When you give me back my gun," Dave said.

Hetzel gave it to him in sections, gun, ammunition clip, bullets, grimly walked him to the door, worked the locks, sent him out into the night alone. Dave went along the lighted cement strip between house and driveway, and when he reached the front corner of the house, heard Hetzel close the office door. Dave started across the lawn, aiming for the dark Jaguar at the edge of the road. The air was heavy with the smell of eucalyptus. Eucalyptus pods crunched under his shoes. And under the shoes of others. He was not alone. Darkness hid them from sight, but they were walking with him.

His heart thudded. It was hard to breathe. Sweat trickled down his ribs. Not breaking stride, he loaded the clip, ignoring how his hands shook. He shoved the clip into the Sig Sauer and jacked a round into the chamber. He didn't put the gun into its holster. It was still in his hand when he reached the dry weeds at the edge of the road, and three of the lads in brown skivvy shirts and fatigue pants stepped out of the darkness to surround him. Their shaven heads gleamed, their perfect adolescent teeth, in smiles that were not smiles. They weren't armed. The only metal he saw was on their feet—steel-toed boots.

"Excuse me, please." He stepped into the street, to go around to the driver's side of the Jaguar. They closed in on him, bumping him with shoulders, elbows, hips. He turned and pointed the gun. There were only two of them. He didn't have time to wonder about that. The arm of the third one closed around his throat from behind. In front, a foot swung up, metal met metal, and the Sig Sauer flew out of his hand. He stamped on the foot of the boy who held him. No good. The choke hold only tightened. He couldn't breathe. His ears rang. His legs went weak. His eyesight dimmed. He was going to black out. A hand rummaged his keys from his jacket pocket, held them up, jingling.

"Let's go," a voice said.

"Yeah." The car door opened. Dave was jerked around, his head pushed down. "Come on, old man. It's time to die."

From across the road, a voice shouted, "Peace officer! Break it up!" A gun blasted. Buckshot whistled overhead. The skinheads yelped. Dave was dropped. Light struck the skinheads, who wheeled in panic, stumbling into one another, and fled in their clumsy boots. Dave pushed to his feet. The light played over him. "You all right?"

Claude Rose came out of the darkness, holding the shotgun. He said, "I warned you not to come here alone. You didn't take me serious."

"I do now." Dave brushed himself off. "Thanks for rescuing me." He reached out a hand. "One more favor, please? Lend me that flashlight. I've lost my gun."

10

◆

Early morning sunlight stretched a long shadow from the sprawling
new house down the flank of a brown hill in a development four miles
out of town. He parked on the road margin in front of a house still
under construction, yard strewn with lumber scraps and torn paper
cement bags. Scattered along the winding, new-laid tarmac streets
out here were other houses like it, but the one with the mailbox on a
wrought-iron post, the box lettered R. ALEXANDER, appeared to be the
only completed house in the development. Ranch-style, low-roofed,
with deep eaves, a flagstone path leading to a front door with
diamond-shaped panes of pebbled amber glass. Except for a ragged
double-trunked Spanish dagger that had probably been here a
hundred years, the landscaping wasn't in. Plastic pipe for a lawn
sprinkler system lay at the edge of the lot. In the driveway, a new,
dark-red Sterling four-door waited with dew on its roof.

In the morning stillness, Dave heard the door chimes ring
someplace far off in the house. This was followed by voices, but he
couldn't make out the words. At last a black girl of high school age
opened the door. She wore puffy stone-washed blue jeans and a
man's shirt and had twisted and tied her hair in complications he
didn't know a term for but which he judged were trendy.

"My name is Brandstetter." He handed her his card. "I'd like to speak to Mr. Alexander, please? It's about the death of Jemmie Engstrom yesterday?"

She eyed him uncertainly, blinked at the card, then gave him a little smile and said, "Wait here, please," and closed the door. "Daddy?" he heard her call.

Dave turned and looked at the unfinished place across the street. How long had it been since anyone sawed a plank or drove a nail there? Some little while. The studs were weathering, turning gray, even beginning to warp in places. The door behind him opened again, and he turned.

The black man standing there wore jogging pants, a Rolex watch, and nothing else. His torso looked like a work of sculpture. How old was he? Maybe forty, but he looked younger, even with the mustache and trimmed beard. The most startling thing about his very good looks was his eyes—hazel, almost yellow. "What can I do for you?"

"I'm investigating the shooting death of Vaughn Thomas in Los Angeles last Sunday," Dave said. "The woman he'd been living with, Jemmie Engstrom, was killed here in Winter Creek yesterday afternoon."

Alexander nodded. "I heard about it. It's sad and it's shocking. But I didn't know her, Mr."—he glanced at the card he'd got from the girl—"Brandstetter. I didn't know either of them. Nor the man who killed her—Craig? And I'm short on time. I have to drive my children to school."

"Like Craig, Vaughn Thomas was connected to George Hetzel's outfit," Dave said. "You do know about Hetzel."

Alexander's expression had been one of amiable curiosity. It hardened. "Anyone of my color knows about the Ku Klux Klan. He was Grand Dragon of the Klavern here. He and his sheeted brethren called on me on my first night in this house."

"I heard about that," Dave said. "I'm sorry. It surprised you, did it?"

"These days, I'm a consultant in consumer psychology, marketing strategies, mainly in audio components. But I began as a university instructor. I don't follow politics. Yes, it surprised me. I thought Winter Creek was far enough from the city so it would be free of violence. That's why I came down here with my children and my father to live."

"Not your wife?" Dave said.

"My wife was killed in a random drive-by gang shooting near USC, where she was an instructor."

"I'm sorry," Dave said.

"That was what made me throw up my own teaching career and move down here." Alexander looked past Dave at the untroubled sky, the enduring hills, and thought his own thoughts for a moment. Then he looked at Dave with a glum smile. "Apparently there is no place free of violence. Not for me and mine. It follows us."

"I heard about the dog," Dave said, "the children. You said you'd be driving them to school—where?"

Alexander glanced at his watch. "Up the freeway to Fortuna. There are a few African-American children in their system. There's racism there too, I don't fool myself about that, but Alice and Andy don't draw the special attention there that they drew in Winter Creek."

Dave studied the troubled, handsome face and said, "But it's too late for your father, isn't it?"

The odd eyes looked at him, startled.

Dave said, "He was the watchman at the low-cost housing development that burned. Am I right? A Mr. Alexander."

"Barrett." Alexander nodded. "Barrett Foley Alexander. He'd been a sharecropper in Alabama, went North to work in the Detroit factories in World War Two, and came to California after that. A determined, hard-working man no amount of adversity would stop. In Los Angeles, he took pick-and-shovel work, day laborer—it was all he could get. Later on, he was a school janitor. We didn't have good clothes, and we didn't live in comfort, and sometimes there wasn't much to eat—but somehow he saw to it that all four of his children went to college, Mr. Brandstetter. Two are attorneys, two were university professors—one still is."

"You're comfortably off here," Dave said. "He didn't have to take that watchman's job."

"For his own pride's sake," Alexander said. "He didn't want to be beholden to me for his keep, as he put it. He wanted to pay his way, as he'd paid his way all his life."

"It cost him his life," Dave said.

"It was murder," Alexander said grimly, "and George Hetzel will pay. I won't rest till I've proved that in court. I'll finish him, if it costs me my own life."

"I interviewed Hetzel last night," Dave said. "He swore up and down he had nothing to do with that fire."

Alexander's nostrils flared. "Did you believe him?"

"Not then. But thinking about it—after the ruckus he raised opposing that project, wouldn't even Hetzel, crazy as he is, realize that if it burned, he'd get the blame?"

Alexander drew breath to answer that, then decided against it, smiled determinedly, and said, "We were having breakfast." He stepped back and motioned Dave into the house. "Will you join us? I don't know what use I can be to you, but we'll share a cup of coffee. And you can meet the children. There's time for that." He closed the door and turned Dave an odd smile as he did so. "It will be a novelty for Alice and Andy. We don't get many visitors."

Moving like an athlete, a dancer, with easy and unconscious grace, he led the way through a vast living room, through a long dining area with sliding glass doors that looked out on a sparkling blue swimming pool, and into a handsome kitchen. What the builders probably called a family room lay beyond, full of sunshine.

The girl sat at a table where bowls, glasses, mugs, cereal boxes, frozen waffle boxes surrounded a pot of yellow chrysanthemums. Alexander was clearing a place for Dave to drink his coffee when a twelve-year-old boy came into the room. His head was concealed in a man-sized safety helmet, his thin young body in a camouflage outfit much too big for him, cuffs rolled up, sleeves rolled up. And in his hands was a paintball gun. He pointed the gun at Dave.

"K'pow," he said in his high child's voice. "K'pow."

Dave looked at Alexander. The man was stunned. His voice was thunder. "I told you not to touch that stuff. Put it back, Andy, right now." He started for the boy with a hand raised. "Right now, you hear me?" The boy, with a yelp that wasn't really frightened, that played at fright, stumbled and flapped out of the room. His father called after him, "It's time for school. Hurry up." He gave Dave a rueful smile and shook his head. "You never know," he said.

"Vaughn Thomas was killed playing paintball," Dave said.

"I haven't played in months. Last year, some of us teachers got up a team," Alexander said, "but after Virginia was shot, I didn't feel the same about it."

He brought a glass coffee maker from the stove and filled a mug for Dave. "Anyway, I wouldn't have tried to go alone. Those fields don't welcome blacks."

Dave sipped the coffee. "And you weren't up in Los Angeles last Sunday?"

Alexander's eyes widened, narrowed. "I was. So were several million other people." He pulled out a chair and sat down hard, scowling. "What are you insinuating? I told you, I never heard of Vaughn Thomas."

"It's a routine question, Mr. Alexander," Dave said mildly. "Nothing personal. There aren't a lot of electronics manufacturers in Winter Creek, so that has to mean you travel some. Was it business that took you to Los Angeles?"

"My elder sister, Anne Alexander-Lloyd, a juvenile court judge, became a grandmother last week. We went to see the new baby. There was a celebration."

"And you were late," Alice said. "Out jogging someplace all morning. We nearly starved. Everybody looking at their watches." She grinned at Dave. "Daddy cooks the evilest barbecued chicken in California. Only where was he?"

"It wasn't that late." Alexander glanced nervously at Dave. "You exaggerate. I got a little bit lost, is all. I don't know that neighborhood. Culver City. What kind of a place is that to live, anyway? In the MGM back lot."

Dave said, "And yesterday afternoon?"

Alexander blinked. "What?" Then he understood, and didn't much like it. "I'm a suspect in the murder of Vaughn Thomas, and that makes me a suspect in the death of his wife? Aren't you forgetting? They've arrested Craig for that."

"I'm not forgetting," Dave said. "It's a weak case."

Alexander snorted. "All right—I was at Newport, the marina. For a one o'clock lunch with a client. The Old New Bedford Lobster House."

"The client's name?" Dave said.

"It doesn't matter," Alexander said. "He didn't show. He did telephone the restaurant, after I'd sat there waiting half an hour, to say he couldn't make it."

"And did you take the call?" Dave said.

Alexander shook his head. "The maître d' brought me the message. So I ate in solitary splendor, did a little shopping in those overpriced boutiques, and drove back just in time to get Alice and Andy from school." He frowned. "When did it happen—to the Thomas girl?"

"Around three thirty," Dave said.

"That was when Daddy picked us up," Alice said. "You should see the beautiful jacket he bought me."

"Shoulders big enough for a football player." Andy came in, out of uniform. His hair was cut flat on top, Mike Tyson style. "Girls wear the goofiest stuff."

"And boys get goofy haircuts," she said.

Dave waited up the street and watched the red Sterling leave. When it was out of sight, out of hearing, he went back to the lonely house. He'd noticed as he left that the sliding glass door of a room in the wing facing the swimming pool at the rear was open. He had only to pick a padlock on the wooden gate to the patio, walk around the pool, and step indoors. From the scattering of Nintendo boxes on the floor around the television set, he judged it to be Andy's room.

He crossed the room into a hallway and after a false start found Alexander's den—desk, computer, printer, copy and fax machines.

He looked over the desk, put on reading glasses to scan the contents of a file folder marked FBI that lay there, penciled with telephone numbers and names. Alexander had written twenty letters demanding information on the department's investigation of Hetzel in connection with the fire that had killed his father. The replies had not been forthcoming. But the date on Alexander's latest letter was only a couple of days old—he was still trying. Other folders here were marked *Sacramento, Sen. Cranston*, HUD. He didn't bother with them. He tried a file cabinet. The top drawer held nothing useful. He tried the second and third drawers without luck, rolled the desk chair over, sat on it, and opened the bottom drawer. Here lay a large, brown envelope, no label on it, only scrawled telephone numbers— one for Channel Three in Los Angeles, the place where Vaughn Thomas last worked. His heart bumped. He pulled papers from the envelope, and blinked. Xeroxes of personnel forms, headed ARYAN AMERICA MOVEMENT. He smiled. Hetzel was mistaken. It hadn't been the FBI that had broken into his office to conduct that unauthorized search. Each form had an ID photo. The boyish face on the first form he'd never seen, but the typed name under it made it *Vaughn Thomas*. The form told him little he didn't already know. But Alexander had scribbled two dates at the top of the sheet—21 May 1976 and 13 July 1977. He looked at the next sheet. *Jemmie Engstrom*. He slid the pages back into the envelope, dropped it back into the drawer, closed the drawer with his foot, scooted the chair back to the desk, and quickly opened and shut the drawers of the desk. Nothing.

He left the room, found what he took to be Alexander's bedroom, and searched the closet there. Andy had stuffed the camouflage suit back carelessly. Dave probed beyond it. He pawed around on the closet shelf. Nothing. He went through dresser drawers. Still nothing. Damn. Could it be in the car? He didn't think Alexander would chance that. Police stop blacks too often for no reason except that they're black. In the hall he noticed a ceiling opening. He got a chair, stood on it, pushed up the trap. The rifle was there.

◆

Carrying the carton of cigarettes, he went around to the back, where
the big white hens stalked clucking in dry grass, ragweed, foxtail,
and where sunflowers had toppled from the weight of their heavy
heads. Morning glory twined on a shaky fence and showed purple
blossoms to the new day. A hen hunkered down in the dust, kicked
dust up under her wings, rustled her wings with satisfaction, and
fussily groomed her feathers with her beak. He stepped up on the
rickety wooden stoop and rapped the screen door that rattled in its
frame. Nobody stirred in the kitchen. Making blinkers of his hands,
he peered through the sagging black mesh. Stove, cupboards, table,
and chairs, but no Fern Casper. He called, "Hello? Anybody
home?" But no one answered.

He went around to the front porch and here he didn't bother
knocking. She wouldn't hear over the racket. He stepped into a little
entry hall, then peered into the room the sounds came from. Old
green roller shades covered the windows, so it was hard for him to
see at first. Then he made her out, seated small and shrunken in a
massive overstuffed chair, staring at the brightly colored moving
images of a big, new television set. Packing materials were strewn
over the dusty carpet. A big shipping box stood between him and her.
He moved it with a foot and edged around it. Holding out the carton
of cigarettes, he shouted over the laughter, shrieks, and hectic
applause of a game show.

"Miz Casper? Good morning."

Her cropped head jerked up, eyes wide. She fumbled in the chair,
found the remote control, and aimed it like a lethal weapon at the set,
and picture and noise died.

"Good morning," she said, and waved a hand at the set. "Look
what happened. Those damn fools at the drugstore made a mistake,
and I ended up with a brand new television. I tried to tell the boy, but
he wouldn't listen. Says it was for me. Barges in here, unpacks it,
wires it all up. I expect he'll be back before long to take it where it's
supposed to go. I'm trying to get some fun out of it first."

She blinked in sudden surprise at the cigarettes. "Oh—are those
for me?" He gave them to her, she began clawing at the carton to get
it open. "It's my lucky day, isn't it?" She cackled happily, pushed

up out of the chair, headed for the kitchen. "Come on. We'll have coffee to celebrate."

When the coffee steamed in thumb-smeared white mugs on the table, and cigarette smoke circled their heads, she said, eyes bright with tears of happiness, "Oh, I tell you, I've missed my television. Time you get to my age, everybody dies on you, you know. Or else they're old and crippled up like me and can't go anywhere without a wheelchair and a nurse to push it and a tank of oxygen standing by. It gets lonesome."

Dave remembered Max Romano again, and changed the subject. "What did you learn from nosing around the neighborhood?" he said.

Her wrinkle-webbed face went blank. "About what?"

"Did anybody see who entered Barney Craig's house yesterday afternoon?"

"Oh, that." She twisted out a cigarette, and right away lit another from a crumpled paper matchbook that advised her to enroll in classes that would teach her to drive a truck. EARN BIG MONEY/BE YOUR OWN BOSS. She pretended to study the printing for a moment, then looked at him slyly, and grinned with her snaggly teeth. "You thought I forgot, didn't you?"

"You're pretty good at teasing," Dave said.

"Used to drive the boys crazy with it," she said. "My mama said if I didn't stop, none of 'em would marry me." She chuckled and drank some coffee. "And Mama was right—none of 'em did." She reached suddenly across the tabletop and squeezed his hand. "I shouldn't tease you about the TV set. Thank you. It was you that sent it, wasn't it?"

"You're welcome," Dave said. "What did you learn?"

"It was a feller dressed like a jungle fighter, ran up on the porch and straight inside, middle of the afternoon."

"Your witness didn't recognize him?"

Fern Casper shook her head. "Might have been any one of them from over at Hetzel's—that's how she put it."

"Did she hear the shots?"

"She did, but she was in the bathroom by then, didn't know

where they came from. Didn't figure it was him. He didn't have a gun with him."

"He didn't need one, did he?" Dave said. "Barney has guns enough for a small army in that house."

"I've heard that." She nodded.

"She didn't see him leave, then?" Dave said.

"His car was gone, time she looked again."

"What kind of car was it?"

"Little gray one. Common. She says its the kind you get when you rent one at an airport." She peered at Dave through the smoke. "That any help to you?"

"She didn't say whether he was tall or short, fat or thin, young, old?"

Fern Casper smiled again, proud of herself. "I figured you'd want to know that. So I asked her." The smile faded. "But all she said was, average, nothing special."

"Could he have been black?"

She eyed him, startled. "You talking about Ralph Alexander? No, he drives a red car. Something new and fancy, English, somebody said." She waited, and when Dave didn't comment, she added, "You can't tell what color somebody is when they wear those helmets."

"Where had you seen his car before?" Dave said.

"Over there," she said. "At Barney's. Monday morning."

11

◆

"How in hell did you find a witness?" Claude Rose said. He sat at a gray metal desk in his glass-partitioned office at the Fortuna County sheriff substation, ate an Egg McMuffin, and drank coffee out of a paper cup printed with yellow arches. "Me and Underbridge asked every householder on that street. Going in, I knew we wouldn't get noplace. Barney's Hetzel's man—and Hetzel's got everybody scared."

"I used a technique I learned in World War Two. I traded cigarettes for information."

The goose-necked man stared. "You're kidding."

"A little old lady trying to live on Social Security," Dave said. "Harmless. She'd get the gossip if I asked her to and I asked her to and she did. I doubt you'll get out of her who the witness was, but does it matter?"

"Doesn't seem to," Rose said, "not much." He wiped his mouth with a tiny paper napkin, crumpled the napkin, the sandwich wrapper, and the paper sack the sandwich had come in, and dropped these into a wastepaper basket. He asked, "Anything interesting in it?"

"When I went to see Hetzel last night," Dave said, "a gray compact was parked in his driveway."

"A zillion cars like that." Rose shrugged. From a desk drawer he took a pipe. An old suede tobacco pouch lay on the desk. He took off it the large paper clip that held it shut—the zipper had evidently given up—and poked shag into the pipe's scorched bowl. He lit the pipe with a long lick of flame from a throwaway lighter. Aromatic smoke drifted in the office air. "And he was dressed in camouflage and a helmet? Might have been anybody? Might have been Barney, then, Brandstetter."

"Did you check? Was he in L.A. on Sunday?"

Rose ducked his head in a nod and smiled a smug little smile. "He was up there, all right. Receipts on all them illegal guns and bullets I seized out of the cupboard where the boy hid show that. He took delivery on 'em on Sunday, drove 'em down in his truck."

"What's he want with them?" Dave said.

"Hell, they ain't his. Barney won't talk. Ain't said one word, not even to his lawyer. But the way I figure, he was just holding 'em till Hetzel could take 'em off his hands. Once Hetzel would have had Barney deliver the stuff to him direct. But he's cagy, now. Lutz, the sheriff here before me, he looked the other way, and Hetzel laughed in my face at first, but I put a stop to those hoodlums of his going around town armed, and he won't warehouse guns and ammunition with me watching. He claims he's a big patriot, and I'm impeding the defense of this country from enemies—"

" 'Within and without,' " Dave finished for him.

Rose gave a quick laugh. "You know how he talks." He sobered, took the pipe from his teeth. "No, Barney was up there, and he could have done it, blended in, like you says, with the rest of the players at that there Combat Zone, with a real gun, and blew Thomas's head off, and nobody would have been the wiser."

"He could have. But I have a problem with it. What's his motive?"

Rose moved his narrow shoulders in a shrug and drank coffee from the paper cup. "They got so many secrets out there at Hetzel's, it could be anything. Something Thomas knew he couldn't be trusted to keep quiet about? Who knows?"

"But if Barney was going to kill Jemmie, why not kill her in L.A.? If he knew where to find Vaughn, he knew where to find Jemmie.

Unless she knew he killed Vaughn, what reason had he to kill her? And if she knew that, she wouldn't have run to his house to hide, now would she, sheriff?"

Rose wagged his head. "Beats me. Makes no difference, one way or the other. He's in for possession of illegal firearms, if not for murder. I'm hanging on to him. You got a better suspect for me?"

"What about Ralph Alexander?" Dave said.

Rose's eyebrows rose. "You serious? I know he blames Hetzel for his father's death, but—"

"He was up in L.A. Sunday morning and can't account for his time. Yesterday, he claims to have eaten lunch out at the marina, the Old New Bedford Lobster place. The staff there should be able to confirm it, if it's true. But he still could have stopped off for a brief two minutes at Barney Craig's on his way to pick his children up from school. And he owns a camouflage outfit."

"And a red car."

"Isn't there a Hertz or Avis office in Fortuna? I'll bet there is. He could have rented the little gray car after he dropped the kids off at school in the morning, and returned it before he picked them up in the afternoon." Dave lit a cigarette, blew smoke away, said, "He lied to me this morning when I went to see him. Claimed he didn't know Vaughn Thomas or Jemmie Engstrom."

"And he did?"

"I saw pictures of them both at his house, and he paid a visit to Barney's place the morning after Jemmie got there. That red car was seen parked outside."

"You don't mean it." Shaken, Rose laid down his pipe. "But why would he kill her? Why would he kill Thomas?"

"To frame Hetzel," Dave said. "He's getting nowhere trying to prove Hetzel was behind his father's death. Maybe he ran out of patience."

"Dear Lord." Rose rocked back in his chair and rolled his eyes at the ceiling. "What next?"

"He also owns a rifle. Large-caliber. Hides it in the crawl space under his roof." Dave stood up. "Since Barney isn't talking, ask

little Mike what Alexander wanted, when he paid that morning call."
Dave stepped to the door, reached for the knob, turned back. "Any
sign of Engstrom yet?"

"Not a sign," Rose said, and his smile was weary. "But I'm not
going to let it trouble my mind unduly. This case is enough of a
mare's nest already." Dave swung open the door, and Rose sat
forward. "Do me a favor, Brandstetter. Don't pull any more fool
stunts like last night."

"They weren't going to kill me," Dave said. "They were only
trying to scare me out of town."

"Maybe—in an ambulance." Rose grunted. "But maybe in a
hearse. They're mean, my friend, no conscience at all. Take you out
to some deserted place and kick you to death? They'd enjoy the hell
out of that. Word has it, Hetzel keeps 'em on a short leash. Way I
figure it, that's a good way to turn 'em even meaner."

Dave twitched a grin. "Why didn't you arrest them?"

"Because I was alone, and I value my hide." Rose lit the pipe
again and smiled slyly. "You want to press charges?" He leaned
back in his creaky chair and blew a smoke ring. "I'll form a posse
and go round 'em up."

Dave shook his head. "Let's save the taxpayers' money," he said,
and left.

◆

He drove along Persimmon Street. Because Barney Craig wasn't
talking, Dave needed another look inside his house. But a deputy sat
tilted back on a kitchen chair on the porch. It was Bob Lowry, the
baby-faced kid Dave had met at the hospital last night. He was in
uniform, hat pushed back on his fair hair, and he was reading again.
Dave walked up the cement strip to the foot of the porch steps. Lowry
heard him and looked up from the book. It was a thick book, and its
shiny jacket said it was new. "Mr. Brandstetter." Lowry's child
eyes searched Dave for damage. "You all right?"

"Your boss told you, did he?" Dave said. "How I was rousted by

Hetzel's storm troopers last night, and he rescued me?" He climbed the steps. "What's the book about?"

"Vietnam—what a shuck that was." Lowry closed the book and laid it on the porch planks. "Everybody lied. Everybody was rotten. Right from the start, right from Kennedy on."

"Politics is a profession of liars," Dave said. "Why are you here?"

"Rose asked L.A. to send a forensics team to go over the house to see what we missed, only they got busy and"—Lowry read his watch—"they won't be here till three." He grimaced. "I hope they make it. This gets boring."

"Then everything's still the way it was?" Dave said.

"Everything but the body and that ammunition dump of Craig's off the back porch."

"I'd like another look at the house," Dave said. "I won't disturb anything."

Lowry frowned, doubtful. "I don't know . . ."

"You can come with me to see that I behave."

"Okay." Lowry sighed, let the front chair legs down, stood up. "It'll make a little break in the monotony." He opened the screen door, unlocked the house door, stood back for Dave to go in ahead of him.

"Thank you," Dave said. "Now when your children ask you, 'What adventures did you have when you were a deputy sheriff, Daddy?' you can tell them about this moment."

Lowry grinned and closed the doors. "I don't think they're old enough to stand the excitement."

The place was very still. It smelled faintly of beer, cigarette smoke, Mexican food. Dave pretended interest in the living room, where the outline of Jemmie Engstrom's small twisted corpse was still bold on the worn carpet. In the dining room where, like Neil O'Neil, Barney had his office, typewriter, calculator, racked rolls of blueprints, table strewn with invoices, files in pasteboard boxes made to look like big, thick books. In the kitchen, where an old refrigerator buzzed, and a sheet of taped-down plastic covered

Mike's bloody little footprints on the lusterless linoleum.

But he wasn't interested in these. Nor the hallway, the bathroom, Barney's room, where boots and sweat socks and locker room smells mingled with whiffs of Clarice's perfume, and the sheets on the open bed were in a lavender and pale-pink floral pattern, with ruffled pillow cases. No, what he wanted to see was the room Jemmie had occupied.

It was at the back, separated from Barney's by the bathroom. She had unpacked a few things—comb, hairbrush, blow drier, jars and bottles of cosmetics, not many, nothing fancy. But the dresser drawers were empty. She hadn't unpacked her clothes. The suitcase stood on the floor at the foot of the bed. He laid it on the bed, zipped it open, searched it. Nothing but clothes. He closed it, set it back where it had been, and looked around, frowning. Lowry, leaning in the doorway, asked:

"What's the matter?"

"Where's her handbag?"

"I don't know." Lowry came into the room and opened a closet with no clothes in it except for a cheap flannel bathrobe hanging on a hook inside the door. It looked as if it had hung there unused for years. A cross pole held empty wire hangers. A pair of dried-out work shoes lay on the closet floor. On the shelf above lay a dusty, collapsed basketball. He took it down, put it back, looked at Dave.

Dave said, "She left Los Angeles with a suitcase"—he knocked it with his shoe—"and a large, over-the-shoulder handbag." He knelt and looked under the bed. Dust and balls of fluff and the cellophane from a long-ago pack of cigarettes. "Now, where the hell is it?"

Lowry tilted his head, puzzled. "Why does it matter?"

"Because when the police in L.A. searched her apartment, there were no papers—letters, bills, receipts, check stubs, bank statements, licenses. She was in a panic to get out of there, running for her life, yet she stopped to gather up the papers. Why?"

"Doesn't make sense," Lowry said.

"It made sense to Jemmie," Dave said. "That's why it matters. The papers aren't in the suitcase, so they must have been in the handbag. And if the handbag is missing, then that was what the killer came here for."

"Bills, receipts, canceled checks?" Lowry scoffed.

"Not those," Dave said. "Not likely. But papers of some kind, the kind worth killing for. Maybe Thomas kept all his papers in one place—a drawer, even a big envelope. People do. They make a habit of it. It's a way of having everything together come income tax time, but what they won't need goes right in there with what they will. They can sort it out in April. And Jemmie just emptied the drawer or snatched up the envelope and shoved it all into her bag, the worthless papers, and the ones that cost her her life." He stepped out of the room into the hallway. "If that bag isn't in this house, then find the bag, you find the murderer—you can bet on it."

"Maybe she left it on the Greyhound," Lowry said.

"Phone and find out," Dave said, "and after that, if you don't mind, check in Craig's trucks outside."

Greyhound had no such bag in their lost luggage room. The cabs of Barney Craig's trucks were busy with junk, but no over-the-shoulder bag. Dave and Lowry turned out every cupboard and closet, every possible and impossible hiding place in the house and among the building supply storage sheds in the backyard. They spent an hour and twenty-five minutes at it. They didn't find the bag.

"Can I read my book now?" Lowry said.

"I promised you excitement"—Dave pulled open the front door, pushed the screen, stepped out onto the porch again into the fresh country air—"and I kept my word."

"My heart was racing"—Lowry locked the door once more—"with the thrill of it all." He dropped onto the chair, picked up the book. "You're right. I'll never forget it."

"If Barney changes his mind and starts to talk, have Rose ask him if he remembers that bag." Dave stepped down into the sun. "And let me know, will you? I'm at the Ranchero motel." He lifted a hand and made for the street. "Appreciate your help."

"Don't tell Rose," Lowry said. "I could lose my badge."

12

◆

He looked into the New Corral, but the eye-stinging fumes of beer, smoke, and disinfectant that reached him, and the deafening twang of country western music, backed him off. He let the damaged door fall shut. He would have his before-lunch drink in his motel room. He didn't get there. Three blocks on the way, he saw Dallas Engstrom. His spavined pickup truck with the weathered camper on it stood to the side of an Arco station, hood up, steam geysering from the radiator cap. Engstrom had dragged a water hose over to the truck and was playing water from it onto the radiator. His white houseman's outfit was grimy and rumpled. A smear of what might have been axle grease ran down one side of his face. His long yellow hair was blowing in the wind. And the way he moved said he was tired or past tired. Dave drove up beside him, stopped the Jaguar, and got out. When Engstrom heard him, he turned, and was so surprised he almost dropped the hose. He did stop it running. His eyes were bloodshot.

"What the hell are you doing here?"

"I came for the same reason you did," Dave said. "To protect Jemmie. I left after you. Where have you been?"

"Son of a bitching truck." Engstrom kicked its front wheel savagely. A new tire was on that wheel. "Broke down on me five times. Five different times. Five different reasons. Five different little beach towns where you have to graduate in ignorance to run a repair shop. Fucking miracle I ever did get here." He dropped the hose and peered at Dave. "Is she here? Did you find her? Is she all right?"

"Can I see the receipts from those repair shops?"

"What for?" Engstrom's angry blue eyes narrowed. "What are you getting at?"

"I think you got here yesterday," Dave said, "around three, three thirty. I'd like proof I'm wrong."

"Shit." With a disgusted laugh, Engstrom yanked open the cab of the truck, and pawed around on the seat inside for a minute, among candy wrappers, beer cans, hamburger boxes. He swung back to Dave with a fistful of grubby pink and blue and yellow flimsies. Credit card receipts. Dave put on his reading glasses and checked the dates. Yesterday, today. Many miles away from Winter Creek. He gave back the slips. Wordless, Engstrom tossed them into the mess on the truck's seat and slammed the door. "Satisfied?"

"Yes, thank you." Dave pushed the glasses into the leather jacket. "But I wish it hadn't happened."

"You wish. Shit, cost me a fucking fortune. I ought—" He broke into his own thought, tilted his head, asked, "Why?"

"She needed protection, and I was too slow."

Engstrom grabbed him. "What do you mean? What are you saying? Is she hurt? She is hurt, isn't she?"

Dave pried his fingers off. "She went to Barney Craig's to hide. But before I could locate her, someone killed her, Dallas. I'm sorry."

"Killed her!" Under the grease smears Engstrom's face went white. "Mike too? Not Mike."

"Not Mike," Dave said. "He's going to be all right."

" 'Someone' killed her? Who?"

"They've arrested Barney, but I don't think it—"

"Son of a bitch." Engstrom slammed down the hood of the truck, climbed into the cab, started the clattering engine. "He wanted her. He always wanted her." The handbrake of the GM clanked, the engine roared, and shuddering and bucking, it careened off the filling station asphalt into the street. Engstrom's voice drifted back. "He couldn't have her, so the stupid bastard killed her."

"It wasn't that way," Dave said, but with only himself to hear. He stepped back into the Jaguar and followed the pickup. Engstrom drove it fast and almost out of control, veering wildly, cutting into and out of the lazily moving vans, pickups, produce trucks that made traffic at noon in Winter Creek. A few of them squealed their brakes and stalled and shouted angrily after the camper. At the little town's one half-important cross street, a signal light showed red. Engstrom ignored it, laid a hand on his horn, and barreled across, just barely missing an eighteen-wheeler that roared a hoarse diesel honk after him.

Dave was no longer up to that kind of driving. Once, long ago. How many company cars had he totaled chasing or being chased by the likes of Dallas Engstrom in the course of forty and more years? No more. He was too old. It was aggravating, it was humiliating, but there it was. He waited for the light to turn green. This meant he pulled into the parking lot of the sheriff substation only in time to see Dallas Engstrom yank open a glass door and run into the building. He was shouting. An AK-47 assault rifle was in his hand. Pulling the Sig Sauer from its holster, jacking a bullet into the chamber, Dave ran after him.

A hallway with doors on both sides went from this side entrance straight to the reception area. Dallas stood there in a half crouch, gun pointed. "Take the gun out, put it on the floor, and kick it over here," he said.

"Engstrom?" Dave couldn't see him, but the voice belonged to Sheriff Claude Rose. "Where the hell have you been? What do you mean coming in here with a gun? Don't you know the trouble that's going to make for you?"

Engstrom roared, "Shut up. Do what I say."

Back against the wall, Dave moved along the hallway, trying to keep the cowboy boots from making any sound. He held the gun up beside his hat brim, ready.

"Are you crazy?" Rose asked Engstrom. "Don't you know any minute now a deputy back from lunch is going to walk in that door you got your back to and shoot you down?"

"Give me the gun!" Engstrom bellowed, raised the barrel of the AK-47, and fired. The shots came fast. Dave thought he counted five.

"All right," Rose yelped. "Here's the goddamn gun."

Dave heard the sheriff's revolver hit the floor, heard it skitter across the sleek vinyl tile. He crouched and ran along the thirty remaining feet of the hallway and was in the reception area when Engstrom bent to pick up the revolver. He pushed the barrel of the Sig Sauer into Engstrom's right kidney and said, "Drop the gun, Dallas." Out of the corner of his eye, he saw the sheriff come from behind the desk and start toward them. Then Engstrom reared back with a roar, something struck Dave above the ear, and he was on the floor, stunned, blinded. He felt the pistol torn from his fingers. He struggled to speak, to get up. No good.

Boots clattered, Engstrom shouted something about keys, the sheriff shouted back at him, a steel door clanged. His head hurt. He touched the place. His hand came away bloody. He pushed to his hands and knees, head ringing. Behind the inner door back of the sheriff's desk was a barred jail door. Now this was open, and pushing the sheriff ahead of him, Engstrom was making his way among empty cells. "Barney, you son of a bitch. Where are you? I'm going to kill you like you killed my wife."

Dave tottered to his feet, stumbled around back of the counter, and grabbed up the headset of the dispatch radio. He peered at the machine. It wasn't big or complicated but it took him a costly few seconds to dig out his reading glasses and find which buttons did what. Meantime there was a lot more shouting in the cell block.

"Get ready to die, ol' buddy."

"Will you shut up and listen, you dumb bastard?"

"Come to your senses, Engstrom. This ain't the way."

"I didn't kill her, Dallas. It wasn't me."

Dave said into the microphone, "Emergency, emergency. Sheriff station. Man with a gun has the sheriff hostage." The front door opened. Dave looked. The young man who came in was tall and wore suntans and a badge. He had a thin beak of a nose and little stupid eyes. He blinked surprise at Dave. He came for the counter. "Put that down. Who are you? What the hell do you think you're doing?"

Dave pointed at the open door. "In there. Watch out. There's a man with an AK-47. He's got the sheriff hostage."

Underbridge, it had to be Underbridge, squinted where Dave had pointed, and took steps toward the door.

"You'll need your gun," Dave said.

"Oh, really?" Underbridge sneered. But he did take the gun from the holster on his hip. He went to the doorway, stood back to the wall beside it, peered around the door frame, as all law enforcement officers are trained to do. "Jesus," he said to Dave with raised eyebrows, "it's true." Then he stepped into the doorway, knees bent, gun held out straight in front of him with both hands, and yelled, "Peace officer. Freeze. Drop your weapon or I'll shoot."

"Not unless you want me to drop your boss."

"I'm giving you one more warning." Underbridge stepped through the doorway now, still with his gun held out. "Drop that rifle or I'll shoot."

The AK-47 spoke. Underbridge staggered. His gun went off. Engstrom yelled in pain. Underbridge collapsed, groaning, clutching his midriff, curling into a fetal position on the floor. Then Dave heard Claude Rose.

"All right. That's that, now, Engstrom, God damn it." Dave heard a clink, the snap of handcuffs. "Look at the mess you made." Rose backed into view, his own gun restored to its holster, the Sig Sauer tucked into his belt, the AK-47 in his hand. He must have fastened Engstrom to cell bars, but he was watching him all the same. He stepped over the fallen deputy, knelt by him, touching him gently, giving him quick glances but keeping Engstrom in his sights. "Underbridge? Let's see. Ah—damn. It's okay, son. You'll be okay." He stood up. "Brandstetter? You out there?"

"I'll call the ambulance," Dave said.

In an aseptic room with small children's bright paintings taped to one white wall, a doctor young enough to be his grandson clipped and shaved a place above Dave's ear, cleaned the cut made there by the barrel of Engstrom's rifle, stitched up the cut, wrapped bandages around Dave's head. While he did these things, he spoke in a quiet voice, almost a hum, the drowsy sound of bees in clover.

"What was it?"

"Assault rifle," Dave said.

"Gives a new twist to the word," the doctor said.

Dave said, "What about the deputy?"

"Abdominal gunshot wounds are tricky. Can't say." He stitched. "Engstrom has a shattered forearm." He took another stitch. "You're taking this very calmly."

"It helps to know it's the last time," Dave said.

"How's that?" the doctor said.

"I'm retiring," Dave said. "This is my last case."

"What are you—FBI or something?"

"Death claims investigator," Dave said, "for insurance companies."

"I thought that meant pushing papers."

"I spend more time like this"—Dave winced as the last thread tightened and the doctor snipped it—"than pushing papers." The doctor took his arm, helped him off the table, sat him on a molded plastic chair. Dave said, "Insurance companies are the richest in the country, the most powerful, the greediest, and the most ruthless."

"Tell me about it," the doctor said wryly, "I'm an M.D., remember?" He poured orange liquid from a covered plastic pitcher into a paper cup. "You should have my insurance rates." He handed Dave the cup. "Excuse me—you were saying?"

"Just that now and then some otherwise sane citizen thinks he can rip them off." Dave swallowed the liquid. It tasted like orange juice, but not much. "Thank you." He handed back the cup. "My job, when murder is part of the scam, is to expose him. And when I start that, he can get mean, and put me in the hospital, and often has."

"Go to bed for the rest of the day," the doctor said. "You lost blood, so drink plenty of liquids and eat well." He made jottings on a form, clipped it together with the admittance waiver Dave had signed, carried it to the room door. Hand on the knob, he said, "If your head aches, take aspirin." He pulled the door open. "There's no concussion. You'll be all right." He went out into a corridor. "Come back in a week to have the stitches out."

"I don't live here," Dave called.

The answer drifted back. "Any doctor can do it."

Blood had run down and dried on the leather jacket and soaked into his shirt and stained his Levis. He bought a brown safari jacket, red wool shirt, and chinos at the K mart store, changed into them at the motel, left the Sig Sauer there, and returned to the hospital, where he found Charlie Pratt on his bunged-up old knees, fitting cowboy boots onto the small feet of his grandson. He looked happy. Mike sat on the hospital bed. He was dressed in a brand new checked flannel shirt, Levi pants, and a brass-button jacket. A cowboy hat was on his head. He held and fiddled with the Transformer toys Dave had given him, while the teddy bear lay beside him, legs in the air. How did Mike look? Happy, no. Unhappy, no. Lost, yes. Waiting, yes. But now he saw Dave and brightened a little.

"Look at me," he said. "I'm going to ride horses."

"Around here"—Charlie Pratt, taking hold of the bed to help himself, creaked to his feet—"they call themselves cowboys when all they ride's a bar stool." He picked Mike up and hugged him. "But you're going to be a real cowboy."

Mike's hat didn't fit because of his bandages. It fell off. Dave picked it up and handed it to him. "That's going to be fun," he said. "I'd like to be you."

"No," Mike said, with a sad shake of his head. "I don't have any mother."

"You've got a grandpa, though," Dave said. "You didn't have a grandpa before."

Mike frowned. "What happened to your head? Did somebody shoot you too?"

Dave smiled. "I ran into something." He hoped no one had told the child what his father did this afternoon and what happened to his father. He guessed they hadn't. He guessed even Charlie Pratt didn't know. He said to Mike, "It's nice you can leave here, isn't it?"

"I guess so," Mike said in a small voice. "But I wish Dallas would come. I'd like to go home."

"You're going to live with Grandpa Charlie, now. You'll like it, I promise." Charlie Pratt set Mike on the bed again. "Tell you what—if you want, you and me can sleep out in the stables with the horses."

Mike said warily, "Horses are pretty big."

"They won't hurt you. They'll be in their stalls, and we'll be in our bunks. But it's nice to hear them breathing in the night, moving around. Nice to smell them. No nicer smell in the world than horse."

Mike nodded and forced a little smile. "I guess so."

"You bet." Pratt gave him a friendly poke in the tummy with a gnarled finger, and he obliged with a giggle, and Pratt saw that Dave wanted to speak to him, and they went out into the hallway. "What's the matter?"

Dave told him about Dallas Engstrom.

"Dear Jesus," Pratt said. "It's all coming apart at once. No mother—now a father in jail. On a murder charge."

"It may not be that bad," Dave said. "The deputy may pull through."

Pratt gave a skeptical grunt. "Why didn't she listen to me six years ago? Now look at that poor little kid. What kind of substitute am I for a mother, for Christ sake?"

"The loss will wear off," Dave said. "He'll forget her in time. And soon you'll be the only person in his life."

"Yup—that's the way it goes, all right." Pratt sighed. "But then what? How much time have I got left, shape I'm in? I could die any time now. Then what happens to him? And if I do last till he's old enough to take care of himself, I'll be used to having him around, and he'll take off like Jemmie did, and then what'll my life be?"

"Stop thinking so far ahead," Dave said. "Enjoy him while you've got him."

"You're right. Thanks." Pratt moved across the hallway to look through one of those glass doors into the patio, where the afternoon sun put leaf patterns on the tiles and on the walls. "You know, I did the same to my old man, same damn thing as Jemmie. My name is Charles Darwin Pratt, you know. My father was a high school teacher. He expected me to go to college and become a scientist, biologist—so did I. What he taught me fascinated me. I couldn't get enough of amoebas and plant cells through a microscope. I memorized the Latin names for everything alive, read every word Darwin ever wrote. Then I got on horseback for the first time. And never wanted to get down. That ended science for me. Instead of going to college, to the old man's disgust I became a stable boy."

Pratt shook his head.

"Never a thought for how it made him feel. Never crossed my mind he had any feelings. But it hurt him, all right. I know that now, just how miserable it made him—miserable as it made me when Jemmie left." His glance at Dave was grimly self-mocking. "She was crazy about horses from the time she could toddle. Lived, ate, slept, dreamed nothing but horses, which you can imagine suited me fine."

He laughed a sad laugh.

"Then, all of a sudden, it wasn't horses anymore. It was boys. She was pretty, and they knew it, and they told her, and it turned her head in a way I couldn't believe. She was so sensible, down to earth, no foolishness. And good and kind and thoughtful and cheerful and loving. We got along wonderful well. And all of a sudden we was strangers, nothing to say to each other. Overnight, Brandstetter, I swear it—overnight."

"Mr. Pratt?" The plump nurse who looked like a choir singer came. "We need you to sign some papers at the desk."

The little man snorted. "And empty my wallet, I expect." He started off with the plump, white woman, then turned and asked Dave, "Will you tell Mike I'll be back?"

Dave nodded and crossed the hall. Mike was on hands and knees under the bed, running the toy tank, buzzing it across the very clean vinyl tile. Dave guessed the sparks it shot out looked brighter in the shadow of the bed. The buzzing stopped. Mike turned the gun turret on the top of the gray toy. "Blam," he said. He turned the gun forward and said, "blam," again, and to the left. "Blam."

Dave was crouched down, looking at him. "Your grandfather will be back in a few minutes. He's very happy you're coming to live with him. You like horses, don't you?"

Mike looked sobered by the question, and thought for a moment before he answered. "Yes. But I like giraffes and rhinoceroses better."

Dave tilted his head. "Those are African animals."

"I know. Vaughn brought a video home." Now Mike came on hands and knees from under the bed, stood up, and faced Dave at eye level. "He was real excited. He said he was going to get a lot of money soon, and then we were going to Africa to live, and I could see giraffes every day."

"A lot of money?" Dave said. "Where from?"

Mike shrugged. "I don't know, but he's coming when he can. That's what Jemmie said. So you can ask him."

It seemed a long time ago that he'd promised himself that drink. So much had happened. Too much. He felt as tired as he'd ever felt in his life. He wheeled the Jaguar into its slot at the Ranchero motel, remembering as he got out and locked the car that he hadn't eaten today. No wonder he was tired. But he couldn't face food. Not now, not yet. He limped wearily down the cement strip with its roof overhang to the door of his unit, turned the key in the lock, pushed the door open, stopped.

He flattened himself against the wall beside the door and reached under his jacket for the Sig Sauer. He didn't have it. He'd left it behind here when he'd changed his clothes. Heart thumping, he waited. He strained to hear, but inside the room no one spoke, no one moved. On the street, cars passed noisily. A stereo raved rock music in a nearby unit. Other tenants ran television. Crows flew over, cawing, black against a cloudless sky, flapping their way from one stand of towering old eucalyptus to another. In starchy white jacket and pants, pushing her cart of towels and sheets, one of the young Latino women who cleaned the rooms came out of a breezeway and stopped and stared at him.

"*Qué pasa?*" she said. "Is something wrong, señor?" Her eyes were dark and glossy. They studied his bandages. "Are you all right?"

"This is my room," he said. "Someone's been in it while I was out. Maybe they're still in it."

Before he could stop her, she passed him and stepped through the door. "*Madre de Dios*," she said. "Why does it look like this? Who would do such a thing?"

Dave looked into the room. Drawers had been pulled out of the chest, dumped on the floor, bottoms smashed out. Sheets and blankets had been torn off the bed. The phone had been crushed to pieces, the television tube shattered, and the machine thrown into a corner. The Johnny Walker bottle was smashed. The long mirror over the chest was slivered. Someone had cut himself. Blood stained the washroom basin, and scrawled under a double lightning bolt in dribbling red on the shaving mirror was: GET OUT OF WINTER CRIK OR DY.

The maid said, "It was not like this before. I clean the room at eleven." She looked up at Dave very earnestly. "I tell you the truth, señor. It was not like this."

"Of course not," he said.

"And I didn't see nobody, nothing," she said. "Nobody seen nothing, señor." She looked over her shoulder, as if invisible agents of evil might be lurking here. "How could they get in?"

He reached across the tiled shower stall whose grout a thousand travel-grimy lather-splashers had turned from white to brown, and slid open the frosted glass of a small high window there. "They must have got in this way. From the back. There's nothing but scrub land out there. And they wouldn't be seen from the street."

"But why, señor?" She was staring at the bloody words, but Dave guessed she couldn't read them. "People who would do this thing—what have such pigs to do with you?"

"Nothing." Dave remembered the heating vent low down in a corner. The grill had been unscrewed and lay on the floor. So the Sig Sauer he'd hidden there was gone, wasn't it? No need to look. "They want me to go away." he said. "What do you think?" He gave her a smile. "Shall I go, or stay and make them pay for this? What would you do?"

She frowned, crouched, and picked up the telephone, the fragments of the telephone, its insides trailing out. "How is this possible?"

"With steel shoes," Dave said.

She dropped the phone and stared. "Skeenheads?"

He said, "I think so."

"Oh, *sí*, go away." Nodding hard, she backed toward the open door as if being near him put her in danger, which maybe it did. "Go quickly, señor—that is what I would do."

13

◆

They walked out of the Channel Three building to the parking lot that was on two terraces carved out of a hillside in Elysian Park. Once, long before the coming of Dodger Stadium, this had been a ragged wilderness of trees, steep slopes, deep ravines where a few frame and shingle cottages crouched, hidden from the world. He tried to remember now the name of a bearded college kid he'd slept with briefly one long-gone summer who had a shack up here and was writing a paper on "The City of Dreadful Night." It was before the war. Dave was still in high school. How he'd met that lean, earnest, bespectacled youth he couldn't think. But to get to his shack, you had to cross a shaky wooden footbridge. He remembered that clearly. He must be tired. Asleep. Dreaming. He pulled the keys from the K mart safari jacket to open the Jaguar, and Cecil took them away from him.

"You're dead on your feet," he said. "I'll drive."

Halfway down the hill, Dave said, "Why did Ralph Alexander telephone Channel Three?"

"I don't know who Ralph Alexander is," Cecil said.

"Sorry, I'll tell you in a minute," Dave said, "but can you ask in your advertising department about that call?"

"I will," Cecil said.

"Alexander had written a lot of telephone numbers on an envelope in his files. As you can imagine, that one jumped out at me. The envelope had material in it concerning Vaughn Thomas. His family home address was on it, and the phone number. Also those of his last employer. Maybe Alexander tried the Steven Thomas house first, got nowhere, so he tried Thomas Marketing to catch him at his workbench—those numbers I wouldn't recognize. But someone at the office, maybe Neil O'Neil, told him Vaughn was at Channel Three, and Alexander tried to reach him there."

"And you know because I told you"—Cecil stopped for a red light—"he hated picking up his phone himself."

"Which I hope means someone took a message," Dave said.

"Right. What time frame are we talking about?"

Dave shrugged. "Start with last week."

The light turned green, Cecil crossed the intersection. "What would this Ralph Alexander want with Vaughn Thomas?"

"That's what I'm asking you to find out," Dave said.

"Okay. Now—who is Alexander?"

Dave told the story as they sloped onto the Santa Monica Freeway and headed west behind an endless curving train of red taillights into the setting sun. Miles later, he finished. "The gun, the camouflage suit, his being in L.A. Sunday morning, the visit to Craig's place, the shaky alibi for yesterday afternoon—and the way he lied to me—"

"Makes him sound like suspect number one," Cecil said.

"Not yet," Dave said. "I need more."

Cecil threw him a small ironic smile. "You need more—or you hate it being him because he's black?"

Dave grunted. "You know me better than that. I need to know about that telephone call. And about two dates Alexander wrote on Vaughn's sheet in that envelope. That's why I'm here. Those dates mean something."

"Did you figure I thought you were here because those skinheads scared you off?" Cecil took the sharply curved ramp down to La Cienega Boulevard. "I do know you better than that. I wish you were a coward. Every time you show up in bandages, I wish it again. But"—he sighed and swung into the traffic heading north for West Hollywood and home—"nothing's going to change you. Only be warned. If you're even thinking of going back to Winter Creek, I go with you."

"No way," Dave said. "You're the wrong color. If you show up there, George Hetzel's storm troopers will do things to your testicles that street kid from Santa Monica never even dreamed of." Dave turned him a tired grin. "And that would upset me no end. Don't even consider it."

Cecil didn't look at him. He watched his driving, but he scowled through the windshield. "So you are going back?"

"Not if I don't have to." The cross street was Beverly Boulevard, and Cecil started to move the Jaguar into the left-turn lane, to head for Laurel Canyon and home. Dave said, "No. Let's go to Max's."

"Ah, Dave." It was a quiet protest. And loving. Cecil knew it was no good to keep stirring up old memories, wakening the ache Dave felt over the loss of the old restaurateur. And other losses that loss kept bringing to mind. But he knew sensible arguments at least for the present had their limits, and he bleakly kept out of the turn lane. When they'd driven on a couple of blocks, he asked, "What dates?"

Dave told him, "May twenty-first, nineteen seventy-six, and July thirteenth, nineteen seventy-seven."

"And they connect to Vaughn Thomas?" Cecil swung west off La Cienega. "But how? He was only twenty-one, Dave. Back then, he'd have been a little kid—what, eight, nine years old?"

"About the time his mother died, and his father married a woman he didn't like," Dave said. "Neil O'Neil thinks it was to try to regain his father's attention that Vaughn desecrated Jewish cemeteries in high school, painted swastikas on fraternity houses in college. The jealous, sorrowing, panicky child crying, 'I miss my mother. I'm all alone. Look at me. Look what I'm doing. Punish me. Anything. But show me you know I'm here. Care about me.' "

"You think he started even earlier?" Cecil said.

"Alexander wrote those dates down for a reason," Dave said. And then he saw the familiar brick-and-beam front of Max Romano's restaurant, and his heart nearly stopped. Plywood panels covered the stained-glass windows. An X of planks crossed the door. A mound of smashed plaster and splintered wood blocked the sidewalk by the driveway. CLOSED FOR REMODELING read a long white banner flapping from the eaves. "Dear God," Dave said. "Already?"

"I knew we shouldn't come here." Cecil shifted gears, started to speed away.

"No, wait," Dave told him. "Drive in, please."

"Dave, why torture yourself?" Cecil said. But with a grim sigh he braked the Jaguar, backed it, swung it into the driveway, drove along the deep side of the restaurant and into the parking lot.

It was empty except for one car, a late-model bronze Accord, parked near the faded red trash module that always stood beside the kitchen door. The trunk of the Accord was open. The kitchen door was open. Cecil put the Jaguar beside the Accord. And out the kitchen door came Alex Giacometti, carrying a large cardboard carton.

Gaunt, pockmarked, fiftyish, with caved-in cheeks and hollow eyes, Alex had been Max Romano's chef for decades. Back when Dave first came to Max's, Max himself still did much of the cooking. But success soon made this impossible. Max's charm and infectious good humor were needed out front. And a day at a time, by slavishly hewing to Max's legendary ways with pastas and cheeses, breads and sausages, meats, chicken, fish, tomatoes, onions, garlic, oregano, basil, and all the other simple ingredients of which mortal cooks could make no more than food, but with which Max made magic, Alex came to rule the kitchen. Now he stopped and stared at Dave.

Dave stepped out of the Jaguar. "You're not leaving?"

"Forever." Alex went, gloomy as a priest conducting last rites for his father, and set the heavy carton in the trunk. Dave stepped closer. The carton was heaped with packets of grubby file cards held by rubber bands, and with loose-leaf binders, soiled and splotched from years of use, pages sticking out, edges tattered. Recipes. Extensions of Max's self. And Alex's. Alex slammed the trunk and sighed. "This is the end. I will never come back here." He started again for the kitchen door, stopped, turned, frowned. Alex had a powerful frown. It had cowed generations of pastry and salad chefs, pot boys, waiters. Even Max, at times. "What are you doing here, Mr. Brandstetter? It's all over. There is no more Max Romano's. *Finito, finito.*" He pulled shut the broad, steel-clad kitchen door and locked it.

"You going to cook someplace else?" Cecil said. "Tell us where? We'll come there."

Alex snorted a laugh, with no humor in it. "No, you won't come there. I'm going back to New Jersey. Why not? The kids are grown. California kids. They'd freeze to death in New Jersey. But I—I like it, my wife likes it, we've missed it all these years. We've saved our money. Maybe I'll miss working, so I'll open a little place of my own. Maybe not. Maybe I'll rig up a hammock in the backyard and listen to the birds. In the fall I'll rake the leaves, pick apples, listen to the rain on the roof. In the winter I'll shovel the snow off the walks, go inside, kick off my galoshes, hang up my coat, light a fire in the fireplace, look at the TV." He climbed behind the wheel of the Accord. His starved, sad face peered out at them. "It will be a dream come true." He twisted a key in the ignition, the car started quietly. "I can't stay here," he said in a suddenly changed voice, and tears glazed his sunken eyes. "Not with how they're wrecking Max's. I know it's nothing. Only a restaurant. There's a million restaurants. Who remembers?"

"I remember," Dave said.

"Me too." Alex nodded gloomily, and began backing the car into the vacancy of the parking lot. "And it hurts, Mr. Brandstetter. No use lying about it. It hurts."

"I wish you'd think it over before you go," Dave said.

"Goodbye, Mr. Brandstetter," Alex said, and steered the car toward the driveway. "Goodbye, Mr. Harris."

And he was gone. Another one gone.

Dave was so tired when they reached the canyon house that he didn't give another thought to eating. All the energy he had left went into taking a shower and dragging himself up the raw pine stairs to the sleeping loft. Cecil had poured him Glenlivet and set the glass on the pine chest. He touched the whiskey to his mouth and found he didn't want it. He dropped onto the bed, stretched out, shut his eyes, sighed. Cecil drew the sheet and blankets up over him. He was dimly aware of that. The next moment he was asleep.

He woke at sunrise. Sitting up, swinging leaden feet to the floor, he knew he needed more rest, another six hours at least. But he had places to go. So he shaved and dressed instead, gave a gentle nudge to sleeping Cecil—face in the pillow, one long arm out of the bed, hand touching the floor, one long, pink-soled foot sticking out where he'd untucked the sheet, as he often did in a bed not built for sleepers well over six feet tall—and went downstairs.

He scooped up mail that had accumulated on his desk and carried it across the leaf-strewn bricks of the sunny courtyard to the cookshack. There he started coffee, laid big country sausage patties in a cast-iron pan over a slow fire, mixed batter for cornmeal pancakes, sat down with a mug of coffee and a cigarette, put on his reading glasses and began sorting the junk mail from the real mail.

The ratio was something like ten to one. Lively little Amanda, his father's last widow, young enough to be Dave's daughter, sent a postcard from Chicago, where she was attending a home decorating convention. Years back, when she'd felt lost and useless after Carl Brandstetter's death, Dave had set her to fixing up this place. She'd done it with sense and style and soon had a thriving business going for her. She was a good friend, and he missed her when work kept her away for any time at all. He missed her now, and read the postcard twice before he laid it aside.

A letter from Ray Lollard, a telephone company vice-president, Dave's friend from high school days, whom he often saw and had never stopped liking, was briefly personal—Ray's antic, wild-haired lover Kovaks was being honored for his pottery by some society or other in New York—but the letter was mainly devoted to a bid for "another of your wonderfully generous gifts" to help rescue some sandy-floored beach-town gallery of arts and crafts, whose collapse was certain "if something isn't done immediately." Dave chuckled to himself and shook his head. Half of these places he was certain only Ray had ever heard of. But Dave would send the check.

He laid the letter aside and frowned. Now, what was this? His name and address were scribbled in pencil in what was unmistakably European handwriting. He knew the style from his time in Germany. Only this looked not just spidery but drunken. He tore open the dime-store envelope. The pages had been crammed inside any which way. He wedged them out, sorted them, flattened them on the tabletop, frowning. The date was Monday. *Dear Mr. Brandstetter, I am sorry. I have tried to telephone you for hours but no one answers. Excuse me please. I also tried to telephone the police. I could not make them understand. You see, I have done a great wrong, and this surely has caused terrible injury to Jemmie. I am afraid she is dead and it is my fault. I am afraid he has killed her. When she ran away, she begged me to tell no one where she had gone. And I kept my word. When you asked, I told you I did not know. I am sorry.*

The screen door of the cookshack creaked. Cecil came in, wearing a white terry cloth robe, towel around his neck, fresh from the shower. Dave pulled the reading glasses down on his nose and looked at him over them. "I had a hunch he was lying," he said.

Cecil went and looked into the mixing bowl on the counter. "Whoa, flapjacks." He poured coffee into a mug and brought the mug to the table and sat down. "Who was lying?"

"Kaminsky." Dave rattled the misfolded pages at him. "There was no phone in the Thomas apartment, but Kaminsky told me Jemmie had phoned for a taxi. She'd used his phone, hadn't she, the manager's phone? A nice, kind little man, an emergency? Of course. And told him all her troubles while she waited for that cab."

Cecil said, "You didn't learn the Thomases had no phone till later."

"All the same," Dave said, "I sensed he was lying, and I should have worked on him till he told me the truth. Jemmie would be alive, Mike would have his mother." He slapped the pages with his knuckles. "Kaminsky would be alive. I'm slipping, young Harris. I'm no good anymore."

"You going to talk rubbish," Cecil said, and pushed back his chair, "I'll cook the pancakes."

Dave read the rest of the letter. *But then in the night I saw out my window this light flickering around in the empty apartment. And I went softly up there, and with a flashlight a man in those spotted coveralls and helmet so I could not see his face was searching. I started to go and phone the police, but he heard me and caught me. He had a gun and put it to my head and asked me where Jemmie had gone. At first, I would say nothing, but then he said that already he had killed Vaughn Thomas, and he would be in no deeper if he killed me, and I broke down and told him. He left at once, and then it was I tried to telephone the police, but they did not understand me, and then you, but there was no answer.* By now the handwriting had grown loose and sprawling and was hard to read. *I have betrayed that innocent girl. He will kill her. Why is it in my life so often I have been forced on pain of death to do contemptible things? In the camps, then after the war, lies to survive, lies to cover lies. But I am not a murderer, Mr. Brandstetter. You must believe me.* And that was the end of it. Drunk and despairing, he'd forgotten to sign his name. One last time.

Cecil laid napkins, knives, forks, spoons on the table, set out butter and maple syrup in a stoneware jug from Vermont. He refilled the coffee mugs, then brought plates crowded with pancakes and sausage, set one in front of Dave, one at his own place, and sat down. "What did he say?"

"That he could have kept Jemmie from being killed, and he didn't." Grimly, Dave unfolded the napkin in his lap. "He had that part right."

"What part did he have wrong?" Cecil said.

"We'll let Sergeant Samuels work that out," Dave said.

The white front of the massive Spanish colonial in Beverly Hills reflected the sun from a clear autumn morning sky. A mockingbird sang one strong note over and over again in a big Brazilian pepper tree down the slope of smoothly mowed lawn. A gray stretch limousine stood on the curved driveway, two fiftyish men in dark suits waiting beside it, talking. Quietly, soberly. These were not types from the frantic world of advertising/marketing. These were mortuary men. Dave's line of work had taken him to hundreds of funerals, and he would know these types anywhere—close up they would smell of mint mouthwash and damp cut flowers. The sight of them swung his thoughts back to Max's funeral, two weeks ago now, but still vivid, still painful. He had to stop remembering. It was too damned sad. He passed the men without looking their way and angrily rang the doorbell with his thumb.

"Brandstetter." Steven Thomas winced against the sun glare. On his bony frame hung a beautifully tailored new black suit. A glass of whiskey and ice was in his blue-veined hand. He glared at Dave. "What the hell do you want? Today of all days. This is the morning we bury the boy."

"I know," Dave said. "I'm sorry to intrude. But I'm still trying to find out who killed him. That matters too, doesn't it?" He stepped inside, took the door from Thomas's frail grip, swung it closed on the shouts of the mockingbird. A couple of tall white wicker baskets holding elaborate flower sprays stood on the tile floor of the entryway beside the twisting staircase. Remembrances from friends? Not Vaughn's, Dave guessed. Sylvia's, probably. "I've got two questions, that's all," Dave said. "The answers won't take any time, and they are probably very important."

"What's important," Thomas said, walking away, shaking his head, tears in his voice, "is my only son is dead, and that finishes me." He wandered to a deep chair in that huge impersonal room and dropped limply into it. He stared ahead of himself at nothing. "That finishes Steven Thomas and any point there ever was to his life. Success? Money?" He snorted irony, then raised his eyes to Dave. "I'm seventy-five years old, Brandstetter. He was only a boy. What kind of justice is there in that?"

"He told Jemmie Engstrom he was about to get a lot of money," Dave said.

"She's alive, then?" Stevens said. "She's all right? Poor little thing. I didn't think she had enough defenses to make it in this world."

"You were right," Dave said. "She's dead. Whoever killed Vaughn caught up to her before I could."

"Oh, no," Thomas said. "Oh, no." He gulped from his whiskey. "I'm so sorry. If Sylvia had just—if I'd only—"

"It was her little son who told me. About this money Vaughn was about to get. A lot of money, he said. Enough to take him and Jemmie and Mike to Africa to live. Where was that money coming from, Mr. Thomas? You?"

"Africa?" Unexpectedly Thomas smiled. "Yes. He had a love for Africa. All his life. Read about it all the time. When he was small, it was the animals, of course. Later on it was the wars. After England and France and the rest of them let those countries have their independence. Vaughn wanted to be part of those wars, get over there in the jungles. A mercenary. Putting his life on the line—not for any cause, just for the adventure of it."

"And the sport of killing blacks," Dave said.

"What? I told you he wasn't like that. How could he be? Growing up in this household?"

"He managed it, I'm afraid. You didn't promise him money?"

"I couldn't if I'd wanted to," Thomas said, and glanced past Dave at the hallway. "Sylvia wouldn't have it. Said he was too young to handle it. I'd always given him whatever he asked. And she was right—he threw it all away."

"As he threw away his mother's legacy when he turned twenty-one?" Dave said. "He gave it to George Hetzel—did you know that? All of it?"

Thomas shut his eyes, shook his head. "No. I didn't know that." He opened his eyes. "Who is George Hetzel?" Dave told him, but Thomas didn't want to hear. He waved his hands. "Not today, Brandstetter. Not this morning. I don't want to remember that side. All that hate stuff. That was my fault. Some way I failed him."

"Some way he failed you," Dave said. He sat on a coffee table in front of Thomas's chair and said, "These dates." He named the dates Ralph Alexander had jotted on Vaughn's personnel sheet. "What do they mean?"

"Oh, get out," Thomas said. "Mind your own business." He

stood up with a suddenness Dave wouldn't have gauged him capable of. Whiskey sloshed from his glass, and cold drops struck Dave's face. "Nineteen seventy-six?" Thomas scoffed. "Nineteen seventy-seven? He was a little child then. What difference does it make what he did?" Thomas crossed to the hall. "He didn't know there was any harm in it. Anyway, what possible connection could it have to his murder?" Dave followed him. "Leave it alone, Brandstetter. Leave me alone." The words echoed in the round stairwell. He raised his head. "Sylvia, are you ever coming down here? You never loved that boy, you never loved him." He didn't wait for a response but yanked open the front door, and still gripping the whiskey glass, went down to the waiting limousine. A mortuary man opened the car for him, he dropped inside, the door slammed. He sat slumped on the rear seat, drinking, staring ahead at nothing, looking very old.

Dave quietly closed the house door. The big white rooms were as silent as if no one were home. Puzzled, he climbed the steps. His soles were soft and made no sound on the tile treads. At the top of the stairs he stopped and listened. Somewhere a voice spoke, low, insistent. Sylvia's. He wanted to talk to her. He looked at three doors, black in the white walls, located the sound, walked toward it, but with his hand raised to knock, he stopped.

"Oh, yes." Sylvia's voice was a trembling whisper. "Oh, God, yes." The whisper grew sharper, more urgent. "Oh, how I've wanted, how I waited, how I—" She gave a low, panting moan. "Oh, my God, yes, yes, no, no, don't stop. Yes, yes. Ah, you're so wonderful, so wonderful. Oh, my lover, oh my darling, oh, yes, oh, yes." Now the words shuddered out of her. "Oh, God, I love—you—love—love—oh—Neil." The last word was a cry. Then there were no more words. Human sounds, sighs, murmurs, soft laughter, not words. Then there was silence.

Dave watched the second hand go around the face of his watch. Fifteen seconds. Thirty seconds. Thirty-five. Forty. Then there was rustling, and he felt under his feet their feet moving on the floor beyond the door. "All right, now," Sylvia said, "you still haven't answered me, God damn it. Where the hell were you Monday night? You promised you were coming back. And I wanted you, Neil, I needed you. You know how exhausted I was. Completely stressed out, working like a demon for three bloody months day and night on that damned Shopwise campaign. And then it was all over and you swore you'd be here to hold me." Now it wasn't lust but tears that made her voice unsteady. "I needed you. You know how I am. I get so fucking tired of being boss lady, all the responsibility, all the tension, all the fights—I'm a woman, Neil, like any other woman, and I have wants and needs and God help me hungers, and I needed you then, naked and strong to hold me. And you promised you'd be back."

"Sylvia, be reasonable. Haven't I been with you every minute since this thing began? I begged you for Sunday off, and it wasn't even noon before you beeped me in. By Monday night, I was totally wrung out. And I just fell asleep."

"Bullshit," she snarled. "You forgot all about me. You always do. The minute we part, I'm out of your thoughts."

"Wrong. The only thing on my mind was coming back to you. I took a shower, unplugged the phone, and lay down for half an hour. I shut my eyes and, wham, it was morning. That shows you how tired I was."

"Tired of me, you mean. Who were you out with?"

"Oh, please. Sylvia, you're the only woman in my life. Be fair. You know I'm always thinking of you—"

Below, the horn of the gray limo sounded discreetly.

"Oh, God," Sylvia said, "look at the time." The door burst open and she was rattling down the staircase, Neil O'Neil close behind her. "Damn that boy." Both of them wore black. From a small black hat of woven straw, a black net veil covered her face. Dave watched from above as she yanked open the house door and charged out into the sunlight. "He goes on being a pain in the ass even when he's dead." O'Neil pulled the door closed behind him.

The room surprised Dave. There was no bed. It was an office— desks, phones, typewriters, computer, lots of paper, printouts, drawings, photographs. No carpet. Slick pages lay on the drafting table, off prints of a full-page newspaper ad, headlined in red. THE SHOPWISE SUPERMARKET SWEEPSTAKES/PRESENTING THE WINNERS. The list of names and addresses was long. Dave folded one of the sheets and tucked it into a jacket pocket, turned, and saw a tiny, brown, wrinkled Asian woman in starchy white blinking at him from the doorway, folded sheets in her arms.

"Can I help you, sir?"

"I came to see Mrs. Thomas," he said. "But she's out."

"She out." The woman nodded. "Funeral of son. Very sad day, very sad."

"Did you know the boy?" Dave said.

She shook her head. "I work here only short time."

"I see. Thank you." Dave moved to leave the room, and she stepped out of his way.

"Who I say call?" she asked.

"Don't bother." He went down the stairs. "I'll come back." And he too went out into the sunlight. The mockingbird had quit. Dave got into the Jaguar, switched on engine and air conditioning, and sat frowning. Neil wasn't asleep at his house Monday night. Dave and Cecil were there. At least until two A.M., Neil was out. Dave grunted and let go the handbrake. A lie to a jealous woman? Was he really trying to make something of that? Disgusted, he drove off.

14

◆

"At ten twenty-five A.M. last Friday."

On a rough round table in a log-framed booth on Olvera Street, a plate of beef enchiladas steamed in front of Cecil. He spread a stingy paper napkin on his knees, tucked the corner of another in at his throat. Bowls of green and red chili salsa stood on the table. He spooned some of each onto the red sauce and melted cheese that smothered the enchiladas, and added a spoonful of chopped onion.

Dave munched tortilla chips dipped deep in guacamole and watched him with amusement. He was a dedicated eater. Yet he remained rail thin. Cecil picked up his fork, threw Dave a grin, growled, and set about eating. There were three enchiladas. When he'd made away with the first, he wiped his mouth, swallowed some dark Dos Equis beer, and said:

"It was Ralph Alexander, all right. He claimed to be with Status Electronics, upscale audio stuff, Pasadena. You ever hear of it? No, neither did I. Anyway, Alexander claimed they wanted to buy commercial time. Not through any agency. Status would package their own spots. And he had to talk to Vaughn Thomas right away. The deal had to be closed before the weekend. Where could he reach him?"

Dave stopped eating. "He didn't have a phone at that apartment. Oh, no—she didn't give him the address?"

Cecil had filled his mouth again, but he nodded and mumbled, "Vaughn had told her it was private, not to be given out to anybody." Cecil gulped down the food. "But she saw dollar signs and figured it was urgent." He drank some more beer, took a tortilla chip, dipped it in the green mixture, held it dripping over his plate. "It was going to be a very big account, to hear Alexander tell it." Cecil popped the scoop of guacamole into his mouth. "And there was nobody around to ask, so she finally just gave it to him."

"Ah, hell," Dave said. He looked out of the shady booth into the sun where, under gnarled olive trees, tourists in baseball caps, Bermuda shorts, dark glasses shuffled along on sloping terra-cotta tiles between rickety stalls of leather goods and silver buckles, gaudy serapes and woven straw figures, chattering in twenty languages and dialects, pausing to watch painted children in fancy Mexican costumes dance to the music of trumpeters, guitarists, concertina players in silver-embroidered sombreros and boleros. It was not very real, but what Cecil had told him was real, and he liked it a lot less. He sighed, picked up his fork, started on his own enchiladas. When he stopped to cool his throat with beer, he said, "Do one more favor for me?"

Cecil poured the last of his beer from the brown bottle into his glass. "Downtown?" he guessed. "Within a few blocks of here? Which is why we came here to eat?"

"Well, I do have to see Abe Greenglass," Dave said. Greenglass was Dave's attorney, scrupulously upright but of deep cunning and a daunting reputation. Over the years, he'd rescued Dave from scrapes that would have flattened other lawyers. Today, Dave had questions for Abe about Max Romano's restaurant. "But you're right. In the back files of the L.A. *Times*, find me items about small boys in trouble—on May twenty-first, nineteen—"

"It's okay—I remember the dates." Cecil pushed back the bench he sat on and carried his empty plate away. Dave ate. Cecil came back with mugs of coffee and saucers of caramel flan swimming in thick cream. "I'll make Xeroxes."

"Please." Dave used his napkin, laid it down.

Cecil said, "Won't be any name, Dave. Law says the names of children accused of crimes can't be printed."

"I know. I've got another source for the name."

"Not Ken Barker," Cecil said. Barker had retired lately, with the rank of captain. He was another friend Dave missed—even remembering how often they'd got in each other's way, how often they'd disagreed. "He might have got it for you, nobody else. Juvenile records are sealed."

"How about a juvenile court judge?" Dave said.

Cecil tilted his head, cocked an eyebrow. "You never told me you knew any juvenile court judges." Dave looked at his watch. "I am about to," he said.

◆

She was a vast woman, huge breasts and buttocks, a neck thick as an NFL guard's, but handsomely groomed, and clothed quietly and expensively. Dave figured her for at least fifteen years older than her brother. Gray streaked her hair. It added distinction, but not dignity. She was as dignified as possible. She would have been dignified in rags and with her head shaved. Her office was not a judge's chambers in the usual sense. On the walls, among certificates and plaques honoring her past work, were posters from learn-to-read and say-no-to-drugs campaigns. In a glass-fronted cabinet, below rows of books, lay an assortment of children's playthings, balls, stuffed animals, blocks, toy trucks, dolls. On the desk stood a jar of lollipops. A secretary, one of a team of serious-looking young women, white, black, Latino, Asiatic, from a large front office, announced him, went out, and closed the door.

"Sit down, Mr. Brandstetter." Anne Alexander-Lloyd's voice was deep, authoritative, but a splendid smile tempered its tone of command. He took a slimly padded leather-covered straight chair, and she said, "Forgive me if we only have a few minutes. I'm terribly busy. It's always that way in September—new school term starting, the troublemakers and the uncomfortable and the misunderstood surfacing in their new surroundings. But I wanted you to come.

I have seen you on television several times and read about you in the magazines, and I always say to myself, or to anyone who happens to be present, 'I knew him when.' "

"Is that so?" Dave was honestly surprised. He couldn't remember everyone he'd ever met, of course, but surely he hadn't forgotten a woman of such thundering presence. He smiled bewilderment. "I'm sorry—when was 'when'?"

She laughed. It was a wonderful, wholehearted laugh. She shook with it. "Well, there you have me. Twenty years ago? Twenty-five? It was in the matter of that poor child with diabetes. Her parents let her die while they prayed over her. What was her name? Phyllis something."

"Gardner," he said, and frowned, "but I still—"

"I was clerking for Judge Wheeler then," she said. "A little bitty slip of a black girl. I expect you didn't notice me. I didn't have much to say for myself. You came to talk with the judge in his chambers, with two men from the district attorney's office. I served coffee. I thought you were the handsomest man I'd ever seen outside the movies." She laughed again. "You still are."

Now he had to laugh. "I'm an old wreck," he said.

"And I," she said, "am no longer a slip of a girl." Laughing again, she took a quick look at her watch, then asked, "You wanted to see me about what?"

"A boy who was murdered last Sunday morning," Dave said. "Not quite a boy anymore—he was twenty-one. His name was Vaughn Thomas."

As quickly as her laughter had come, she was somber. Also guarded. "I don't believe I know about that."

"I believe you knew about him once," Dave said. "In high school he vandalized a Jewish cemetery."

She shook her head quickly. "It didn't come before me."

"Then let's go back earlier, to when he was eight and nine." He gave the dates. "What did little Vaughn Thomas get up to then?"

"You realize," she said sternly, "that what you are asking is privileged information. Juvenile records are closed. Only under very special circumstances, through court orders, can any information in those files be released." She twitched a mocking eyebrow. "You haven't come here with a court order, have you?"

"Did your brother Ralph come with a court order?" Dave said. Her mouth dropped open, but she couldn't find words, and Dave pressed on, "No, I didn't think so. And yet you told him about those dates and what they meant—it had to be you, didn't it? Who else could do it for him? Why would he try anyone else?"

"What do you know about my brother?" she demanded.

"That he wants very badly to find out who it was that set fire to that low-cost housing development in Winter Creek, and caused his father's—your father's death."

She sat very still. "He told you this?"

"Yes. And that he feels George Hetzel was behind the fire. That much he told me. But that he'd come to think Vaughn Thomas was Hetzel's agent, the one who actually set the fire—that I stumbled on myself. I've been slow working it out."

Her smile was thin. "Have you worked it out?"

"I think so," he said. "Vaughn Thomas left George Hetzel's organization very suddenly only a day or two after the fire. The date was right under your brother's nose, but it took him time to notice it and add up what it might mean. I expect it wasn't until last week that it dawned on him. I don't know what else he learned in that week about Vaughn Thomas's past, but he learned from you about those episodes in nineteen seventy-six and nineteen seventy-seven. And they were meaningful, weren't they, judge?"

"Our father was a very special man," she said.

"So Ralph told me," Dave said, "and so I believe. In his own way, Vaughn Thomas was special too, wasn't he? George Hetzel certainly thought so."

The black woman snorted contempt. Her eyes smoldered.

"What was so special about Vaughn Thomas?" Dave leaned forward in his chair. "It was that he had a lethal tic, wasn't it? He liked to set fires, isn't that right? Isn't that what he did those long-ago summer days after his mother died? Isn't that what you found for your brother in Vaughn Thomas's juvenile crime jacket?"

"I deny that," she said. "Categorically." Those stormy eyes

brooded on him. "You are a formidable man, aren't you? Audacious. Reckless, even."

"Not so reckless I'm not still here," Dave said. "I know whom I'm up against. But I submit that someone shot Vaughn Thomas dead on Sunday morning, that your brother Ralph came to see you that same morning, then disappeared from his family's sight for hours, that he owns clothing that could have got him unnoticed into the paintball playing field where Thomas was shot. And that your brother owns an assault rifle. Add these facts to his well-known determination to track down and destroy the man responsible for his father's death, and I think the district attorney is going to have to ask for an indictment. What do you think?"

She drew a measured breath. "I think my brother is innocent. I know him. He would never take another person's life."

"There's more," Dave said. "The young woman Vaughn Thomas was living with—"

"That's enough." The judge heaved her bulk up out of the chair. Instantly the door behind Dave opened and one of the strict young women appeared. The judge snapped, "Show Mr. Brandstetter out, please. And bring in the Carters."

Dave shrugged into the safari jacket, put into its pockets his wallet, private investigator's license, cigarettes, lighter, and keys, and went down the pine staircase from the loft. His Stetson hung on the hat tree by the bar. He put it on. Cecil came naked out of the bathroom, drying off from the shower with a big yellow towel.

"You leaving already?" he said.

"Where did I put those clippings you Xeroxed for me?"

Cecil had found the stories in the *Times*, all right. Vaughn's first was only a little fire—a vacant lot, an abandoned shed. BOY PLAYING WITH MATCHES STARTS BLAZE. "Released to the custody of his parents." But the second, the following year, ended up charring five hundred acres of brush and trees in a canyon. "Fire fighters were able to contain the wind-whipped flames before they reached the area's expensive homes." How disappointing for little Vaughn. Expensive homes. Just like his father's.

"At my end of the couch," Cecil said. He pulled on jockey shorts. "Let me come with you this time."

Dave retrieved the envelope with the clippings. "I've got a better idea." He walked back to his desk and picked up the off print he'd taken from the drafting table in Sylvia's workroom/playroom. Steven Thomas's voice said in Dave's head, *Can't even climb stairs anymore.* Dave held the folded page out to Cecil, who took it, opened it, ran his gaze over it, frowned.

"What kind of idea? Why better?"

"A human interest story for you, Mr. Producer. The people on that list are suddenly, and by the luck of the draw, richer than they were before. Some of them much richer—look at that, a hundred thousand dollars, fifty thousand, twenty thousand five times over, and on down."

"To a measly hundred," Cecil said.

"It's a better idea for two reasons. First, a man with a job ought to show up for work now and then, and I've kept you away too much already—and second, I came back from Winter Creek with a question I haven't found an answer to."

"Keep talking." Cecil ran up the stairs, long-legged, two at a time. "I can hear you while I dress."

"Vaughn told Jemmie and Mike that he was about to get a lot of money. Did you hear anything about that? Were there rumors around your store?"

"No." The broad bed rattled. Cecil must have sat on it to put on his shoes. "His old man is rich, though."

"His old man wasn't giving him anything," Dave said. "Sylvia wouldn't allow it." Dave paced. "Drugs? Drugs are a source of big money."

"I'd say no." Cecil appeared at the top of the stairs, pulling on a bulky cotton sweater. "Drugs go around anyplace in show business, including the washrooms at Channel Three—or so I hear. I never saw any little plastic packets change hands myself, but you'd have to be blind, deaf, and stupid not to know who's into the scene among my fellow elves." He came down the stairs. "And one of them was not Vaughn Thomas." He took Dave's arm and steered him toward the door. "We're going to talk—it might as well be over coffee." They crossed the courtyard to the cookshack. Plainly, Cecil had been here before his shower, while Dave had dressed—the air was rich with the smell of coffee. He filled yellow mugs and brought them to the table.

Dave said, "If not drugs, what?"

Cecil made a sound, set down his mug, spread open the contest announcement sheet again. He ran a long finger down the lists of winners, blinking over it, sat straight. "No luck. No Vaughn Thomas among the winners."

Dave laughed and shook his head. "He's a member of the family, and for a short time during the Sweepstakes, he was an employee of Thomas Marketing. That rules him out twice."

"So? What am I doing with this list?"

Dave said, "Playing a long shot. The Sweepstakes is the only source of sudden money close to Vaughn I know of."

Cecil said, "But if he couldn't touch it—"

"Let me think." Dave drank coffee, lit a cigarette, turned the slim steel lighter over in his fingers, staring at it, brooding. At last he looked up. "What about blackmail?"

Cecil jerked his head back in surprise. "Whoa. You saying Vaughn knew something sleazy about somebody on this list? But how? He left Thomas Marketing weeks ago. How would he know who the winners were going to be?"

"Talk to Neil O'Neil. Maybe he noticed something while Vaughn was working with him. Maybe it ties to Vaughn's quitting so suddenly." Dave gulped the hot coffee, set down the mug, got to his feet. "Regardless—check out some of the winners," he said. "See what turns up. One of them might play paintball. Ah, hell, maybe it won't answer my question, but it will make good TV." He went to the cookshack door. "Your viewers will love it." He opened the door. "Everybody daydreams about coming into sudden wealth."

"What was Vaughn going to do with it?" Cecil asked. "Give it to Hetzel, the way he did his mother's legacy?"

"Mike said Vaughn told him Hetzel was the enemy," Dave answered. "No—he was going to move to Africa."

"Maybe he got the money," Cecil said, "and that was why he was murdered. Maybe he had it on him Sunday morning."

Dave shook his head. "The payoff wasn't till Tuesday."

"You going to nail Alexander?" Cecil said bleakly.

"Look on the bright side." Dave went back to him and gave him a kiss. "I also plan to nail Hetzel, the Black Man's Friend." And he left the cookshack, smiling.

15

◆

Dave said, "Biggest one-night motel bill I ever paid. Nine hundred seventy-six dollars." He sat in the sheriff's substation in Winter Creek again. The door to the outside was propped open and a breeze came in, smelling of sage and eucalyptus and promising a warm day. "And the room was nothing to speak of. No view at all."

It was breakfast time again. Claude Rose munched a Danish pastry and washed it down with coffee from an outsize styrofoam cup. "And you never even reported it. You should have reported it. I could have took fingerprints. I'd love to lock up them skinheads."

"What I'm reporting is the gun, my Sig Sauer," Dave said. "Hetzel will have it. I want it back."

"What did it cost you?" Rose said.

"That's not the point," Dave said. "It's the only gun I ever owned. I'm against guns. They give too many people power who have no right to it. Guns cancel out intelligence, reason, decency, civility, and put terror in their place. I got along without a gun most of my working life. But a man can't buck the odds forever. About five years back I bought the Sig Sauer. I'm used to it. And I don't know that I'm morally prepared to buy another one."

"For Hetzel to admit he's got it," Rose said, "will be to admit he was behind them that wrecked your motel room. He won't do that, will he? Cost him too much money." Rose sighed. "Hell, I suppose if you say so, I've got to try." He picked up a pencil. "It got a number on it?"

Dave recited the number for him and Rose wrote it down. Dave said, "Look at it this way—it's another excuse for you to hassle him without him getting pissed at you, since it's my doing." He lit a cigarette. "How's Underbridge?"

"Still in intensive care," Rose said grimly. "Like they say, guarded. His condition is guarded." He peered at Dave. "How's your head? I see you took the bandage off."

"I forgot about it," Dave said. "And it came off in the shower. I'm not sorry. My hair covers the wound, and I'm spared telling a long, stupid story over and over again."

"Did I thank you for trying to save my bacon?"

"Don't mention it." Dave reached and pulled the glass ashtray across the desk. It was washed and polished and there were no pipe dottles in it yet. "It wasn't one of my better moves. I'm too old for that stuff now."

"I know what you mean." Rose crumpled up the wrapper from the pastry and threw it away. He licked his fingers and wiped them on a little paper napkin and threw that away too. "Biggest lie in the bunch is 'You're as young as you feel.' Hell, I wake up every morning feeling eighteen—right up to the time I ask my body to get out of bed."

Dave said, "Did you question Mike? What did he say about Ralph Alexander's visit Monday morning?"

Rose barked a laugh. "He come about the sprinkler system for his front yard. Seems it was supposed to be in and working before he moved into the place. And Barney Craig was the contractor. And Alexander kept phoning him, putting messages on his machine, but Barney never returned the calls. So finally, Alexander drove by early to catch him and says, 'When are you going to put in my blankety-blank sprinkler system?' and Barney says he's too busy to get around to it, and Alexander better call somebody from over in Fortuna to do the job."

"Because nobody in Winter Creek would be caught dead working for a black man? Least of all Barney Craig, George Hetzel's good right arm?"

"Well, of course, little Mike didn't say that." Rose rattled open a desk drawer and brought out his stem-chewed pipe. Dave slid the ashtray over to him, and he knocked the dottle from the pipe into the ashtray, and then filled the pipe from the worn suede pouch. "But if you was out there to see Alexander, you know his is the only house around that got finished. The developer, Horace Thalberg, is one of Hetzel's heavy contributors. He didn't know Alexander wasn't white until he'd moved down here—the whole transaction was took care of by a Los Angeles bank."

Rose chuckled and lit his pipe.

"It made Horace so mad he damn near had a stroke. I know. He was in here storming around, wanting me to arrest Alexander and throw him off the property for getting it by fraud and misrepresentation. No use, of course. Law says it don't matter what color you are, you can live where you like. So Horace stopped work on the other houses, and put them and the land on the market, because he's convinced nobody with the kind of money them places cost would want to move in next door to coloreds." Rose's pipe hadn't lit well. He used his long-flamed lighter on it. Aromatic smoke clouded the air. "Looks like everybody agrees with him—he hasn't found no takers. But he'll go bankrupt before he'll change his attitude."

"Was Mike in the front room when Alexander paid his visit?" Dave asked. "Did Alexander see him?"

"No. I was particular to ask that. And about his mother, too—Jemmie. No, they was in the kitchen, and the door was shut. No way Alexander could've knowed they was there. And if that don't put him in the clear, I checked out all the car rental agencies in Fortuna. He never rented no little gray compact—not Tuesday nor any other day."

"I'm relieved to hear it," Dave said.

"Me too," Rose said. "He's one of them people you was talking about—civilized. Met him a couple times. We don't get a lot like him down here. The rich ones, yes, but the bright ones, no. Writes books, did you know that? And George Hetzel—how he'd have gloated if it turned out Ralph Alexander, Ph.D., was a killer. Be proof, wouldn't it, he's been right all along about black people—nothing but animals."

"Unlike those model specimens, Engstrom and Craig."

Rose chuckled and coughed pipe smoke. "And since it was one of Hetzel's boys he murdered, it'd also show the world the blacks were killing off the whites and taking the country away from them, way he always claims."

"Vaughn Thomas was living in fear those last weeks in Los Angeles," Dave said. "Afraid to answer his phone at work. Didn't even put a phone in at his apartment. Told everybody at his workplace not to give out his address."

Rose poked at his pipe with a penknife. "Is that so?"

"You wondered why little Mike wouldn't talk to you at the hospital. The reason was—Vaughn had given him strict instructions never to talk to sheriffs, policemen, or George Hetzel. He told Mike these people were not 'our friends.' "

Closing the penknife with a click, Rose peered at Dave. "George Hetzel too?"

"So Mike said. Why do you suppose that was? Vaughn had been Hetzel's darling. Then, the night after the housing project burned, he took Jemmie and Mike and ran. With not so much as a goodbye. Did you ever wonder about that?"

Rose tilted his head, frowning. "Date never came to my attention. Remember, I only just moved here to replace Lutz about that time. But if Thomas was scared of Hetzel, don't it mean Hetzel was after him? And don't that point the finger right back at Barney Craig? Hetzel wouldn't go himself to try to find Vaughn."

"Hetzel was in Columbia, South Carolina," Dave said. "Delivering a sermon on the text 'Love thy neighbor.' "

Rose jerked a nod. "So he sent somebody, didn't he? And Barney was up there in L.A. Sunday morning, and he sure as hell knows how to shoot a rifle."

"You didn't learn anything about Vaughn when you questioned Hetzel after the fire? His leaving that way didn't strike you as significant?"

"Strikes me as significant now you point it out, but Hetzel's got a lot of young dogs around there, none of 'em house-broke. Vaughn Thomas was just one of the pack, far as I was concerned. I heard stories about him, racing around town in that little red roadster shooting off his gun, stuff like that—but not till later, after I'd settled in here. And he was gone by then, anyway, wasn't he? Now, when you talk about my questioning Hetzel and his troops about the fire, I rounded 'em up all right, but there was so much milling around and yelling that night—firemen, arson experts, lawyers, TV crews, phones ringing from Washington and Sacramento—I didn't get a chance to ask 'em much of anything. And the next morning the FBI moved in, and I kept out of their way. That's how they like it, you know."

"Hetzel's office was broken into shortly after the FBI completed their investigation. Did he lodge a complaint?"

Rose nodded glumly. "He was fit to be tied. I wrote out a report and sent it on over to Fortuna, and I don't know what they did about it. Nothing, I expect. They thought like I did the FBI probably wasn't satisfied, and sprung a midnight raid to try to catch old George out."

"That's what he thinks," Dave said.

Rose blinked. "And you—what do you think?"

Dave stood up. "I don't think—I know." He leaned across and put out his cigarette. "It was somebody else. I can produce the proof. But I'd rather not. Not quite yet."

"If you've got evidence of a crime," Rose said strictly, "it's your duty to share it with me. That's the law."

"I don't have it, sheriff. I've only seen it." Dave walked to the open door, stood looking out at the autumn hills and breathing in the sweet morning air. "But if things work out, it will be in your hands tonight."

"Where you going now?" Rose said.

"To try to work things out," Dave said, and left.

Someone, probably Ralph Alexander himself, had been digging long, shallow trenches in the front, and laying plastic pipe in them. A pickax and spade lay nearby, along with paper sacks of grass seed. But the house in Horace Thalberg's abandoned development among the empty hills was deserted. Dave had figured it would be. It was the time of morning when Ralph Alexander was humming up the freeway in his red Sterling, taking his kids to school in Fortuna. Dave parked the Jaguar in the drive and waited.

Half an hour later, Alexander swung his car into the driveway, braked it noisily, so it was still rocking on its springs when he jumped out of it, and slammed its door. He wore white shorts and a purple-and-white striped tank top this morning, and sandals. He looked muscular and angry. He stalked to the driver's side of the Jaguar and glared with those strange pale eyes of his through the open window.

"What the hell are you doing here?"

"Didn't your sister phone you?" Dave said.

"You had no right bothering her," Alexander said.

"She had no right," Dave said, "giving you that information from Vaughn Thomas's juvenile record." He worked the latch and started to open the door. "Excuse me, please." Alexander backed off, but still glowering. Dave got out. The sun glared in his eyes. He reached into the car and got the Stetson, put it on, let the car door fall shut. "So that makes us even, doesn't it?"

"No, it doesn't. Why are you harassing me and my family? I told you, I didn't kill Vaughn Thomas."

"You also told me you never heard of him, didn't know who he was," Dave said, "yet back there in your workroom is his personnel file, along with those of a dozen other former members of George Hetzel's outfit. You'd not only heard of Vaughn Thomas, you had his photograph, you knew when he joined up with Hetzel, the home he came from in Los Angeles, and most important of all, the date when he left Hetzel."

"You broke into this house?" Alexander's handsome face became a mask of outrage. "You went through my files?"

"As you broke into Hetzel's, and went through his."

Alexander scoffed. "Broke into Hetzel's? That's ridiculous. Have you ever been there? It's surrounded by armed guards. How could I break in there?"

"You've got more brains than they have," Dave said. "You figured out a way. You've got those papers."

"For what they're worth," Alexander said sourly. "I couldn't find anything better. I only took those personnel records of defectors hoping one of them was disenchanted, and could tell me something to use against Hetzel." Alexander laughed ruefully. "Nothing like that. They were just drifters, just moving on in their pickups, with their guns and grenades and paranoia. Thomas was the last in the alphabet. And it took me a long time to make anything of him."

"Then you noticed he'd left Hetzel's the night after the fire, you were alerted by the coincidence," Dave said, "and you began searching for him. Among other places, you phoned Channel Three in Los Angeles to get his address. What did you want with it? What did you want with him, if it wasn't to kill him?"

"What do you think?" Alexander said. "Because I'm black I'm just naturally a killer, is that it?"

"That isn't worthy of you," Dave said. "What I think is that once your sister had confirmed your suspicions that Vaughn Thomas had a pathological fascination with fire, you became convinced he was the underling George Hetzel sent to burn down that housing development, killing your father. You'd been trying to get the FBI, HUD, your senator, anybody in authority to go after Hetzel, and getting nowhere. So you decided to take matters into your own hands."

"You didn't find any documents in my files showing Vaughn Thomas set fires as a child."

"I found the dates when he did it. You wrote those down when your sister told you about them," Dave said. "I checked them out in the morgue at the *Times*." He drew Cecil's envelope from a pocket, took out the copies of the clippings, laid them in front of Alexander, who squinted at them. "No names are given," Dave said, "but on those dates you jotted on your Vaughn Thomas page, a young boy set fires, didn't he? I'm not surprised you don't have the documents. Your sister wouldn't have copied them and faxed them to you. If you'd used them to try to indict Thomas, they'd have been too easily traced to her. Barrett Alexander was her father too, after all. That she'd made unauthorized use of those files for personal advantage would have put her career in serious jeopardy. Anyway, they were weak stuff to try to build a case from against Vaughn Thomas. They probably wouldn't even have been admitted as evidence. And she very likely told you so." Dave eyed him for a moment. "Which shortened your options, right? What was there left to do?"

"Not murder," Alexander shouted. "I tell you, I didn't kill him."

"He was shot with a large-caliber rifle," Dave said. "Like the one hidden in the crawl space under your roof."

"I bought that rifle to defend myself," Alexander protested. "The day after the Klan came calling."

"I believe you," Dave said, "and I don't blame you, but you did take it to Los Angeles last Sunday morning, didn't you? And not for defense. You had Vaughn Thomas's address. After you dropped your youngsters at your sister's, you went on over to Thomas's, isn't that so?"

Alexander shook his head. "No."

Dave went right on. "It wasn't far. But Vaughn had gone out early, hadn't he? To play paintball at the Combat Zone. You faked for Jemmie the same story you'd faked on the telephone to the advertising section at Channel Three that you needed to see him about buying commercial time for—what was it?—Status Electronics of Pasadena. It was urgent. A lot of money was involved. And that's why she told you where he'd gone. And then you went after him."

"No," Alexander said. "I tell you, no."

Dave said, "You had the jungle fatigues in the trunk of your car, along with the rifle, and wearing a helmet with a face mask, you knew, black or white, you couldn't be identified. You tracked him through the woods until you spotted him. And you shot him down."

Alexander kept shaking his head.

"And when Jemmie learned what had happened," Dave said, "she cleared out, afraid you'd come back and kill her too. She took the Greyhound home to Winter Creek—thinking she'd be safely out of your way here. Instead, she stepped directly into your line of fire, didn't she?"

"Oh, stop," Alexander said wearily. "All right. I'll tell you the truth." He trudged off toward the house. "I couldn't tell you the other morning. The kids were here. Come inside." His keys were in his hand. He unlocked the front door, and went in, leaving the door open for Dave. Dave wished he had the Sig Sauer. Heart thudding, he followed slowly, hoping that rifle still lay in the darkness under the roof. Whether it did or not, it wasn't in Alexander's hands when Dave found him in the kitchen, heating coffee. Alexander said, "I was at my brother's. I think I mentioned him to you before. A lawyer? Louis—the youngest of us." Alexander glanced at Dave over a shoulder. "He's gay. Sit down, please. I'll have us coffee in a minute."

Dave went into the family room, pushed cereal boxes, muffin packages, jam jars aside, and stacked some of the breakfast dishes so there'd be room on the table for coffee mugs. He sat down, and looked out at the sun glinting on the pool, and in a couple of minutes Alexander was there with the coffee. He dropped heavily onto a chair opposite Dave, and said bleakly, "It was never a subject you could bring up in the presence of my father. And Anne still doesn't want to hear about it. Oh, she's a sophisticated woman. She knows it's not Louis's fault—that you're born gay or you're not. It's that he told Daddy. That's what she can't forgive."

"Isn't there another sister?" Dave said.

"Arletta." Alexander nodded glumly. "Yes, well—she never had a mind of her own. What Daddy felt, she felt, and Daddy was crushed. He wasn't educated, you know. He thought Louis was sunk in perversion and filth, and until he got down on his knees to God and begged His forgiveness and changed his life, no way was his father going to speak to him again. And Arletta went along with that and she still does."

"Which makes you his only contact with his family?"

Alexander nodded, lifted his cup. "And it hurts him, you know. It grieves him." He sipped coffee. "For all those years we were so close—all of us, and then suddenly, in law school, he makes this discovery about himself, and he's not one of us anymore, he's an outcast."

"But you see him," Dave said. "And that was where you were Sunday morning? That was why you told Anne and the others you'd got lost jogging? To explain why you were late getting back for the barbecue?"

"I see him as often as possible, but I never tell them, never mention his name. It always caused unhappiness, but the way things are now—" Alexander gave a bitter smile. "I wouldn't normally have been late. There was an emergency. When I arrived, Milton was trying to carry Louis down the stairs from their apartment. Louis can't walk by himself anymore. He weighs ninety-three pounds. Louis has AIDS, which means in his case about a dozen different infections. He's out of his mind much of the time." Tears blurred Alexander's eyes. To try to get his voice under control he stopped for a moment and drank from his coffee mug. "They met in law school and they've lived together ever since. I don't know what Milton will do when Louis dies, and he's going to die—any day now, any night. This time it was the pneumonia—it keeps coming back. Milton was trying to take him to the hospital. Again."

"And you went along to help," Dave said.

"I drove them. I suppose you'll want proof, witnesses? Not Louis—a brother will lie for a brother. And Milton, he'll say anything, he's so pitifully grateful to me for any little thing I do for them. But you try that hospital." He gave a brief, dry laugh. "They'll remember me. I'm not like Milton. The staff can walk all over him. He weeps, screams, carries on, but they're used to that, they don't even notice. When I lose my temper, they notice, and they'll remember. Junipero Serra Hospital. You check."

"I will," Dave said. "But none of it changes the real reason you went to Los Angeles on Sunday, does it? You went for a showdown with Vaughn Thomas."

"Well, I didn't have it, did I? And most certainly I did not kill him. Yes, I got that address from the television station, so I could find him and make him admit he burned the project and killed my father."

"If he did, it was on orders from George Hetzel. Thomas got his punishment. But Hetzel is very much alive. Hetzel is a free man. Hetzel is guilty as hell. I think I can prove it, but I'll need your help."

"I'm listening," Alexander said.

16

◆

It was noon when he left Alexander's. He stopped at the filling station where he'd come upon Dallas Engstrom cooling off his rattly pickup truck the other day. He filled the tank of the Jaguar with gas, paid for it, found a gritty coin phone in a dusty blue plastic shell beside the station office, rang the LAPD and asked Joey Samuels to check Alexander's hospital alibi, then rang Cecil's number at work.

Jesus Salcido answered, a squat, good-humored film editor who always wore a Dodgers cap. Dave had met him a few times. "He's out on that supermarket giveaway story," he said now. "About half the winners live in the L.A. area, you know? He's been ringing doorbells all morning. Funny thing. He checked in by phone a half hour ago, and he told Dot Yamada he thinks he's on to something sensational. See, he only found a couple real people, Dave, you know what I mean? Those winners—half of them don't exist."

"You're kidding," Dave said.

"Cecil wants an explanation, right?" Salcido said. "But Thomas Marketing is closed today. Nobody there. The woman who runs it, Sylvia Thomas, Vaughn's mama—the kid who worked here, you know, who got shot?—she's out of town. Finally, Cecil got hold of her assistant. So he's on his way to Burbank now. That's where the dude lives."

"Neil O'Neil," Dave said.

"That's the one," Salcido said. "Cecil took the van, the crew, he's gone to ask him on camera how come so many winners are 'no such address,' 'nobody here by that name.' "

"I'll be fascinated to hear the answers," Dave said. "He can reach me through the sheriff's substation in Winter Creek. Or at Ralph Alexander's house, same town."

"I'm writing it down," Salcido said. "I'll tell him."

"Thanks, Jesus." Dave hung up, crunched over gravel to the Jaguar, and drove up the road to the Twin Oaks Café for lunch, too hungry to worry about how awful the food would be.

A fiftyish, straw-haired woman in faded jeans, hippish and saggy in the butt, pulled open the door of George Hetzel's office at the rear of his house. Chatting back into the room, she rolled down the sleeves of a dime-store checked flannel shirt, buttoned the cuffs, pulled on a thin green windbreaker. "We'll finish up tomorrow, easy. 'Specially if we get them extra girls in. Ruby Nagel delivered a week's eggs today. She'll be free." The woman stepped down to the driveway and halted, blinking through glasses that looked too big for her, at the sight of Dave, splayed against the little gray compact again, being searched again by the pretty skinhead with the tattooed arms. Now Hetzel looked over the woman's head.

"God damn—excuse my language, Nola." He pushed the woman out of his way and came outside. "Brandstetter. What the hell are you doing here?"

"The sheriff says you won't give back my gun," Dave told him. "I thought I'd better ask you myself."

"I told Rose, I'll tell you—I haven't got it."

The skinhead finished his frisking and backed off in his heavy boots, looking, listening. A second skinhead stood by, holding an AK-47 pointed at Dave. His right hand was bandaged. Dave jerked his chin at him, and said to Hetzel, "Have you asked him? He was part of the housekeeping crew that practiced their skills on my room day before yesterday at the Ranchero motel. I'd left the Sig

Sauer there, hidden in a heating vent. He remembered to leave me a note but not to thank me for the gun. Am I to take it he kept it without telling you about it? I thought you believed in strict discipline. Most military commanders frown on looting, as I understand it—unless they get the loot."

Nola stood there gawking, chewing gum, knobs swelling at the hinges of her jaw. "You go ahead on home," Hetzel told her, helping her start down the walk. "And we'll see you tomorrow morning, early as you can make it."

Nola went, but reluctantly, looking back at the drama, if that was what it was. "I'll bring Ruby if I can," she called. "Her eggs'll be all delivered today."

"Yes, you told me," Hetzel called. "Thank you, Nola."

"Goodbye," Nola said. "See you tomorrow, Mr. Hetzel."

Hetzel waved, smiled. "Bless you for all the hard work. And for staying so late too. Don't you ever forget I'm grateful. You'll see. You and I, we're going to clean this country up and give it to the white people again." He swung back, grabbed Dave's arm, and snarled, "Get inside here."

Dave got inside. Hetzel closed the door, locked it, walked to his desk between long tables heaped high with form letters, hand-addressed envelopes, return envelopes with printed addresses. The colorless man in his colorless white shirt and tie and gray business suit trousers waved a hand at this stuff. He said, "Fund raising for an all-out campaign against network television, the sewage the so-called entertainment business is emptying into American homes, day in, day out, morning noon and night, into the eyes and ears of innocent children, women, old people." He slammed himself down into the padded executive chair at his desk. "There's no limit to how low those Jew perverts will stoop to make money. Sex, horror, garbage not fit to feed to pigs." Sunset light from the windows flared red off the very clean lenses of his glasses. "It's got to stop. America is fed up with it. They're not going to take it anymore." He swept his arm to indicate the worktables again. "Ten thousand pieces of mail there, telling decent people how to protest, write the sponsors, the advertisers that keep TV going, tell them to make the producers clean up their act or we'll stop buying their products." He paused to catch his breath.

Before he could start again, Dave said, "It wasn't the FBI that broke into this office and tossed it."

"What?" The change of subject confused Hetzel for a minute. "Oh, back there after the housing project fire?"

"Back there." Dave nodded. "It wasn't the FBI."

"How do you know who it was?"

"I've been finding the answers to questions like that longer than you've been alive. It's how I earn my living. I know who broke in here and went through your files and what he took from them and the use he made of what he took, and the use he plans to make."

"Plans—?" Hetzel lost color. He stared. He licked his lips. Then he took a breath and blustered, "You're lying. He got nothing. Whoever it was didn't find anything. Nothing was missing. I went over it all myself."

Dave shrugged. "He has documents with the ARAMMO letterhead. I've seen them. Not many. And maybe you wouldn't have regarded them as important, even if you'd noticed they were gone when you were cleaning up after the raid. But they prove he's telling the truth, don't they? After all, where else could they have come from?"

"What documents?"

Dave glanced around. "How did he get in here? It's a challenge, this place, isn't it? All those guards with guns? Cast your mind back to that night, will you, please? What happened? My guess is it started with a diversion—right?"

Hetzel looked wary. "Maybe—why should I tell you?"

"Because those documents connect you to that fire and to the murder of Vaughn Thomas, and only I can tell you where they are."

"I wasn't even in California when Thomas was killed."

"Barney Craig was," Dave said. "He was up in L.A. running errands for you. Why wasn't one of them to the Combat Zone to gun down Vaughn before he could tell secrets you didn't want told? Vaughn was bragging he was about to get rich. He was blackmailing you, wasn't he?"

"No," Hetzel said, "and there were no secrets."

"They're in those documents. And they can destroy you."

"I don't keep documents around that could destroy me."

"You should have kept these," Dave said. "Proof that young Thomas was a pyromaniac. Copies of newspaper stories, copies of his juvenile arrest records. Not only did they suggest to you a means of winning your fight against the housing project, they were proof you could use to shift blame for the fire onto him if the case began to look bad for you."

"What?" Hetzel's laugh was scornful. "You're a liar."

"Then why did Vaughn run away right after the fire? No, it wasn't Jemmie's doing. The next morning, you showed him those papers, didn't you? And you turned from a father figure into an ogre, and he raced to Engstrom's to get Jemmie and Mike, and drove to L.A. and hid from you."

Hetzel shook his head stubbornly. "I tell you, I never had any such papers."

"Then where did this man get them?" Dave said. "They're in his files, clipped to Vaughn Thomas's personnel sheet from this office. Can you prove they didn't come from here? How? If you know any law at all, you know proving a negative is next to impossible. And that you had a known firebug in your ranks the night the housing project burned down—do you think the district attorney is going to ignore that?"

Hetzel sat glowering for a minute. "You dog from hell."

Dave smiled faintly. "I told you I still had my teeth."

"You told me," Hetzel growled. "All right, yes, a phone call came. I didn't take it. Barney took it. He listens, hangs up, looks like he's going to pass out. Says it was Horace Thalberg. That nigger, Alexander—he's kidnapped Ingrid, that's Thalberg's daughter, college girl, broke in and snatched her when she was home alone. He was driving off with her just as Horace and his wife swung into the driveway. He was going to rape her, sure as anything. Barney was out the door right then, and yelling for everybody else, and we all piled into vehicles and headed out for Horace's."

"And in the excitement you forgot to post guards here?"

"Who was it that phoned? It wasn't Horace. Nobody was at his house, but at that time we naturally figured he and Doris had gone looking for Alexander themselves. So I laid out a plan of roadblocks and all that, and dispatched patrols to different points of the compass, and we spent the night at it, walkie-talkies, spotlights, the works. Combed the area, woods, hills, canyons. Got nowhere. My command post was a van in Horace's driveway, and next morning, here they come, big as life—Horace and Doris and Ingrid driving up the street looking surprised as hell to see us there. Been down to San Diego over the weekend with Doris's family—wedding or something. Then, to add to it, we get back here, humiliated, dirty, dog tired, and I find the office all torn up." Hetzel poked his head forward. "Who was it, Brandstetter? Who was it made a jackass out of me?"

Dave had to work hard not to grin. "I'll tell you when you give me back my gun."

Hetzel stiffened his spine. "I can't do that. I haven't got it. Nobody here knows anything about it."

Dave got to his feet. "Then we have nothing more to discuss." He moved toward the door.

"Hold it." Dave heard a drawer open, a heavy object knock the desk top. He turned. "Here's your damned gun," Hetzel said. "Now—you give me that son of a bitch's name."

Claude Rose laid down his knife and fork. He sat at a table in the kitchen of his house, with a supper plate in front of him—beef and noodle casserole at a guess, crusty from waiting in an oven longer than it should. Probably a lot of the sheriff's suppers got that treatment. Though neatly kept up, the Rose house was old. However, the kitchen had been done over recently. The cabinets were covered in walnut veneer, with bronze handles. A burner deck was in the middle of the room with a hood over it. Pots and pans hung off racks. The old-fashioned touches were color photos and handmade greeting cards from grandchildren taped to the coppertone refrigerator, and a string of brightly painted gourds next to the back door. Dave leaned beside these and outlined for the sheriff his visits to Alexander and Hetzel and how things now stood. Rose stared up at him.

"You got a hell of a nerve," he said.

"Did you think I hadn't?" Dave said.

"I don't care." Rose yanked the napkin out where he'd tucked its corner into his collar and slammed it on the table. "You didn't have no right, and I ain't going to be dragged into it. You set it up, you carry it through."

"Alone?"

"What's the matter with Alexander? Whole thing was his idea, wasn't it? Get him to stay and help you."

"It's too late," Dave said. "I've sent him and the children to his sister's in Los Angeles until it's over."

"Well, I don't want no part of it."

"You don't have a choice," Dave said. "You insisted I tell you about this matter. And now I've told you. A crime has been committed. Another is going to be committed. You're the law here. You have to make an arrest. That's your job. If for nothing worse, for breaking and entering. What's the matter with you?" Dave jerked out a chair and sat opposite Rose at the table. "I thought you wanted to stop Hetzel. Who's in charge of this town, anyway?"

"I want to stop him," Rose said. "Damn right I do. But if you'd asked me before you set this crazy thing up, I could have told you—Hetzel is in charge of this town."

Dave squinted. The only light in the kitchen came from a low-watt bulb inside a fake kerosene lantern that hung above the eating table. The lawman's eyes were in shadow. "Isn't it a little humiliating to have to admit that?"

"It would be, if it wasn't that the sheriff of Fortuna County, an elected official, who is my boss, admires the hell out of George Hetzel. And so do half the men and women on the board of supervisors, who see to it the budget has enough taxpayers' money in it to pay my wages. So does the county attorney. This isn't just George Hetzel's town, this is George Hetzel's county."

Dave scoffed. "When he tried to get elected to the State Assembly, the voters turned him down."

"The ones who get elected just call themselves conservatives," Rose said. "But Hetzel, he was right out front with his white-supremacy stuff. That's why. The TV news scared them off, running them videos of Hetzel in his white sheet and hood, the cross-burning ceremony he led, them sound bites where he claims the holocaust is nothing but a Jewish lie—all them upstate anchor boys and girls wagging their finger, saying 'shame.' Ninety percent of the people down here think like Hetzel, hate like Hetzel, niggers, illegal aliens, Vietnamese, people with AIDS—you can take my word for it. Ignorant racist rednecks is what they are, but they didn't like the big city folks saying so. The opinion polls showed Hetzel was a shoo-in, but when it come down to it, Winter Creek turned around and voted middle-of-the-road."

"And you're saying if you move against Hetzel—"

"This wouldn't be a move," Rose said, "it would be an earthquake. We're not talking little stuff here, threats, slander, civil rights violations, carrying guns, concealing arms and ammunition. That housing fire was a major crime. Arrest Hetzel for it? Might as well set myself on fire."

"He's guilty," Dave said.

Rose nodded. "No doubt in my mind about it. And that boy Vaughn could maybe stand a chance of proving it—but he's dead. Hetzel seen to that, didn't he?"

"And you're going to let him get away with it?"

"What can I do—Barney knows the truth, but he'll go to the gas chamber before he'll betray Hetzel. And I don't put a whole hell of a lot of faith in them papers of Alexander's. It's plain enough to me what they mean. But he's black, and it's about the murder of a black man, and even if he got the county attorney to go for it, he's got an all-white, mean-minded, right-wing grand jury down here to get past, and who knows what kind of judge it would go to for trial? Look, Brandstetter, I don't have long to go before I retire. I get on the wrong side of these lunatic-fringers, and I can lose everything, pension, medical insurance, bring disgrace on my wife and family."

He hunched forward, craning his long neck, peering at Dave under the hanging lantern. "You want to be responsible for that? What did I ever do to you?"

"Do you want me to be kicked to death by a squad of Hetzel's skinheads?"

"It's up to you." Rose tucked in his napkin again, and picked up his fork. "You started it." He filled his mouth, chewed, washed the food down with a long swallow of milk. "Call it off, Brandstetter. Go home and forget it."

"I can't do that." Dave stood. "You won't help?"

"I'd be a fool," Rose said.

17

◆

The street lamps worked in Horace Thalberg's abandoned development out in the hills. Spaced along curving streets to nowhere, they cast bright circles of light on the new if dusty paving and the ageless roadside chaparral. The unfinished houses—studs, roofs, chimneys, empty window and door frames—stood stranded on their chopped-off hilltop lots under a wide windswept sky strewn with stars—shelters that would never shelter anyone while there was any chance at all that they might have to shelter blacks.

Dave drove on past the dark Alexander house. He looked for cars on all the streets, saw none, saw no cars lurking, lights out, in shadowy coves or behind clumps of brush. He drove the wide, lonely circle again. Satisfied, he swung the Jaguar in at the Alexander driveway, raised the garage door with the signaling device Alexander had left with him, stowed the Jaguar inside. With a whine and a groan, the garage door closed itself. On his way here from Rose's place, Dave had stopped at the drugstore and bought a small cassette recorder. He'd unpacked it in the car and fitted it with batteries and tape. He dropped it in his jacket pocket now, closed the car, entered the house from the garage.

At Dave's prompting, Alexander had left no lights on and had drawn the curtains on all windows except those on the sliding glass doors of Andy's room, facing the pool. He'd also left one of those doors open, and the padlock on the tall plank gate to the pool area unfastened. Dave paused in the hallway, gazed across Andy's room for a moment, then went through the room and out and around the inky, star-twinkling pool, and unlatched the gate. It swung a little in the wind. Its hinges creaked. That would draw attention. Good.

He stood listening for a moment, heard only crickets, and from the distant creek that gave the town its name, the high-pitched chorus of frogs. He went back inside the house and made his way to Alexander's office. He checked the curtains to be sure of their thickness and that they closed well. Then he sat down at the desk, switched on the lamp there, picked up the receiver, and punched buttons on the telephone.

No one answered at the Horseshoe Canyon place. He rang Channel Three, asked for Cecil, waited, and got Dot Yamada, one of the night news desk anchors. She knew Dave. Third-generation American, she was personable, bright, pretty as a peony, tough as a samurai. "He never came back from Burbank," she said. "It got to be three in the afternoon, and we began putting out calls, but no one answered. He's vanished, Dave. Curly Ravitch too." That was Cecil's cameraman. "And Billy Choy." The sound engineer. "Cecil gave me the address of this McNeil he was going to interview, and we sent somebody to check it out. Nobody there. No sign of the van. Jesus left a message for you at the—what's its name?—Winter Creek sheriff's office."

"I've been too busy to check in there," Dave said.

"Dave, where do you think he went?"

"Beats me," Dave said. "Did you notify the police?"

"You bet," she said. "Donaldson did." Donaldson was head of the Channel Three news department. "He's not worried about Cecil and Curly and Billy. He's worried about the van. It's new. It's outfitted with all the latest equipment, and it cost half a million dollars."

"A man of feeling," Dave said.

"The police put out an all-points bulletin," Dot said. "What do you think—did Iranian spies steal it for the technology? Cecil said this was a sensational story. I'm holding a slot open on the eleven o'clock. But he's going to miss the deadline if he doesn't call in soon."

"I'll tell him when I see him," Dave said.

Frowning, he hung up and rang LAPD. But Joey Samuels wasn't there, neither was Jeff Leppard, and no one available knew anything but that the van was missing, along with one producer, one cameraman, one sound man. All units had been alerted. Big, showy truck. It shouldn't be hard to spot. Probably parked by some back street Burbank tavern, the crew enjoying a few beers on company time. Dave doubted it.

He switched off the desk lamp, left the office for a bedroom he judged to be Alexander's. He pulled the recorder from his pocket and set it on the nightstand, laid the gun beside it, and stretched out on the bed to wait in the dark. He waited a long time. The hum of the refrigerator reached him from the kitchen. After a while, it began to sound too loud, and he rose and went to the windows, ran the curtains back, slid open half the glass wall so he could hear the crickets and the frogs again, and the wind in the dry brush. He stood peering out at the sleeping night hills and straining his ears. His watch read ten of eleven. Surely it was time for him to be hearing the engine of an approaching car, jeep, truck, some sort of vehicle. What was Hetzel waiting for? He lay down again. Time dragged. His eyelids drooped. He rolled off the bed and tottered to the bathroom. In the dark he splashed his face and doused his hair with cold water, toweled roughly, went back into the bedroom, but didn't lie down. He stood smoking a cigarette and gazing out at the night. After the cigarette, he paced to keep himself awake. Then to rest his legs, he allowed himself to sit on the bed, and before he knew it he'd nodded off.

He woke with a start and pawed out for the gun. The motion was sluggish, his fingers numb. He fumbled it, and it made a noise. No one spoke, but he heard the hiss of a sharply drawn breath. A floorboard creaked. Hetzel was here. His heart thumped. Damn. He'd depended on hearing the car arrive. And he hadn't heard it, had he? Slowly, cautiously, he eased his weight off the bed. Hetzel mustn't realize he was here—not until the man had those papers from Alexander's files in his hands. He pressed the record key on the recorder, dropped it into his pocket, and moved to the door. The hallway was black and he didn't even see the man. But the man saw him and poked his chest with a rifle barrel. Dave raised the Sig Sauer. A hand smacked his arm down. Fingers closed around the gun and wrenched it from him.

"Thank you," a voice said. Not Hetzel's voice.

Dave squinted against the dark. "O'Neil?"

"You won't be needing this." O'Neil tossed the Sig Sauer onto the bed. "Come on." He gripped Dave's shoulder, tugged. "Down the hall, then left. Move." Andy's room. Dave peered into the shadows. Was there anything here to grab and bring down on O'Neil's head? The television set was too big. A lamp? He was past the lamp when he decided on it. He made to turn, and the gun barrel rapped his head. Right where Dallas Engstrom's had rapped it the other day. This brought on such pain that he changed his mind about trying to fight, and stepped out into the patio.

"How the hell did you find me?"

O'Neil grunted. "Some idiot at Channel Three relayed your message to Cecil Harris on the van's two-way radio, while it was parked outside my house. Loud and clear."

"What have you done to him?"

"He's all right. Too smart for his own good, though. Like you. And it's going to kill you both. And the other guys too. I really hate that. See what you caused, coming after me for killing Vaughn? Why? He was trash."

"After he came back from Hetzel's"—Dave walked along the edge of the darkly glistening pool—"he worked briefly for Thomas Marketing, and he somehow stumbled on the fact that you were substituting false names for real ones on the winner's list in the Shopwise Sweepstakes, and he was blackmailing you. That's it, isn't it?"

"He wanted it to be Sylvia," O'Neil said. "He wanted to destroy her, and he wanted his father to see it happen. It wasn't Sylvia, of course. This thing took brains. I rigged the whole scam right under her nose and she never even noticed." He laughed. "Vaughn was disappointed at that, but he soon figured out that two hundred fifty thousand dollars would make him feel all better again." O'Neil grunted. "Greedy little bastard. Half. He wanted half."

"Nothing greedy about you," Dave said.

"I earned it," O'Neil said. "What tipped you to me?"

"Papers. You'd planned to go right from the Combat Zone to Vaughn's place. He had copies of those winner lists, didn't he, the true one and the one you'd phonied up to line your own pockets? It stands to reason. He'd have to have documented proof to make his threats against you work. You had to get those papers. But something delayed you."

"Sylvia." O'Neil snorted. "The big executive. Without me, she's helpless. She'd promised me Sunday off. What did I get? Two hours in the morning."

"Just time enough to kill Vaughn," Dave said. "And not until Monday night, when the Sweepstakes was a wrap, could you cut free to get to Vaughn's place, break in, and look for the papers, but you didn't find them. Which meant Jemmie had them with her, didn't she? You scared old Kaminsky into telling you where she'd gone, and as soon as you could find an open office, you rented a car, raced down here, used up half a day trying to find Jemmie, shot her, and took back those papers. In broad daylight. That was risky."

"I got away with it," O'Neil said.

"As a matter of fact, you made two mistakes." Dave stopped and faced him. "First, you took away her shoulder bag. She didn't own jewelry or money. What did that leave? The LAPD had searched that apartment and hadn't found one scrap of paper. That was odd. And oddities bother me. You should have left the bag. You weren't thinking."

"I was half out of my mind. It was blind luck I even found her. I'd been searching for hours when little Mike ran out of that house and she came out to drag him back in."

"Mike was your other mistake. He's not dead, you know."

"What?" O'Neil's voice cracked.

"No, he couldn't identify you," Dave said, "but he could tell me

Vaughn was expecting to come into a lot of money very soon. Where from? The timing said it almost had to be the Sweepstakes. But how? That's when I suggested Cecil interview the winners."

"Yeah, right. Okay, enough. Get moving." O'Neil pushed Dave in the chest with the rifle butt. The tiles were slippery. Dave lost his footing and fell. "Get up." O'Neil bent over him. Dave kicked. His boot caught O'Neil in the face. Blood spurted. The rifle spun high into the darkness. O'Neil teetered, waved his arms, and splashed backward into the pool.

Dave knelt to help him. The pool was suddenly blue. The patio blazed with light. A voice said, "Brandstetter—what the hell's going on?" Claude Rose stood at the gate in his rumpled uniform. "Don't do that." He spoke over his shoulder. Lowry crowded past him, came running, and dragged O'Neil from the pool, water streaming from his long hair.

"He doesn't look it," Dave said, "but he's a killer. Handcuff him." And to Rose, "You said you weren't coming."

"I just drove out to see if Hetzel took your bait. He didn't, did he?" Rose twitched a wry smile. "I never thought he would. Alexander's going to have to take him to court for them reports on Thomas to do him any good."

"You thought he'd come," Dave said. "Or you wouldn't be here. Lucky for me you're braver than your words."

"I'm not. Would've kept right on going if it wasn't for that vehicle." Rose eyed O'Neil sourly as Lowry shoved him past, gagging and dripping. "Big new TV van. There's an LAPD bulletin out on that. Stolen. Only how did it get clear down to Winter Creek? And why? And what the hell's it doing abandoned in Ralph Alexander's driveway? I wondered did it have something to do with you, went to have a look, heard your voice over the fence, and—"

Dave went to him. "There were three men in that van."

Rose nodded. "Tied up and gagged."

"Cecil?" Dave stepped toward the gate. He didn't have to. Cecil ambled in. "No need to shout," he said. "I'm fine. A little stiff in the joints is all." A broad strip of adhesive tape was in his hand. He was trying to rub the white stickum from the adhesive tape off his mouth. He worked up a sort of smile. "Do me a favor? Don't suggest any more news stories to me?"

"If you don't suggest any more murder cases to me."

Cecil held out a palm. Dave slapped it.

"Done," they said together, and laughed—but not because either of them thought anything was funny.

There was endless red tape to unsnarl in Winter Creek, so they didn't reach Horseshoe Canyon Trail until almost dawn, and it was noon before the heat of the sun through the leaf-strewn panes of the skylight over the broad bed on the loft woke Dave. Cecil sprawled beside him in long-limbed nakedness, face down, smooth skin glossy with sweat. Dave got up quietly, dragged the blue corduroy robe off the rail, flapped into it, and yawned his way downstairs to shower. Bathed and shaved, he crossed the courtyard's uneven bricks to the .cookshack, where he took eggs and half a ham from the refrigerator Amanda had updated inside an immense old oaken icebox. He placed eggs and ham on the counter to lose their chill, and squeezed orange juice. He drank some from his glass, assembled the makings of coffee and set a burner going under it, then blended butter and flour and milk in the top of a double boiler over a low fire as the basis for a cheese sauce. English muffins. He rummaged these out, fork split them, dropped them into the toaster to wait, then carried Cecil's orange juice across to the rear building. When he stepped inside, music drifted down to him—Chet Baker's trumpet, sweet and bleeding. Dave climbed the plank steps. Cecil lay on his back, hands clasped behind his head, and stared up at the skylight, open now. A breeze came through it. He turned to look at Dave, tears in his eyes.

Dave stopped. "What's the matter?"

"What isn't the matter?" Cecil laughed a wobbly laugh, sat up, wiped the tears with his fingers, reached for the glass. "All those people dead. All the fear and grief."

"It's over now," Dave said. "Try to forget it."

"How have you lived with it so long? I've only been with you a few years, and I can't handle any more."

"I'm sorry. I shouldn't have dragged you in. It seems to happen. I forget it's not your game."

" 'Game?' " Cecil shut his eyes, hung his head, looked up, and said, "Dave, how can you call it a game?"

"You have to call it something," Dave said. "This one was for half a million dollars. A gamble."

"He was crazy," Cecil said. "You know what he did down there? He didn't know where Alexander's place was, so he stopped at the sheriff's station, walked in, and asked."

"He had another reason," Dave said. "He thought I might be there. While you're mourning, count the deputies on duty who are alive because I wasn't there."

"But what if they'd seen the truck?"

"Why did he take the truck anyway?" Dave said. "Nothing could be more conspicuous."

"Because he couldn't fit us all in his car," Cecil said.

"You were three against one," Dave said. "How did he take you all prisoner?"

Cecil shrugged. "He had a gun. He got the jump on us. He made us tie each other up. Inside the van. He taped our mouths. It was weird. Noon. Cars driving by. Stared right at us—I mean, a TV remote truck, what's going on, right? You think anybody stopped? Shee-it."

"O'Neil gauged the world by his own sick standards," Dave said, "and for a while it worked for him."

"He could have been crazier," Cecil said gloomily. "He could have killed us right there."

"Better to do it at midnight," Dave said, "out in the wilderness of Fortuna County, and dump the bodies where they might never be found."

"Except by coyotes," Cecil said.

"Drink your orange juice," Dave said. "Come have your breakfast. Your problem is you're hungry."

From below a voice called, "Hello? Anyone home?"

Dave looked over the rail. Gaunt Alex Giacometti stood against a background of sunlight in the open doorway peering sorrowfully around. Dave went down in the blue bathrobe. Behind him, Cecil turned off the music.

"Alex, good to see you." Dave went down the long room, took Alex's hand. He wanted to laugh, because he had a good idea of why the chef was here. And then, as he and Alex shook hands, Dave saw, three steps off, outside the door, the dignified straight-backed little form of Abe Greenglass, attaché case in hand. Abe wore a dark suit, a dark topcoat, and a hat. Always. When Dave smiled at him and spoke his name, he nodded, but he didn't move to come indoors. He lived by strict protocol, impeccably correct. Abe's presence cinched Dave's sense of triumph. "Please come in," he said, and Abe came in, taking his hat off as he stepped over the threshold. Dave took the hat, helped him off with his coat, said, "Sit down, won't you?" and carried hat and coat off to the hat tree at the far end of the room.

. In jeans and a yellow L.A. Lakers top, Cecil came down the stairs. "Morning, Mr. Greenglass, Alex. Coffee?"

Lawyer and chef sat in the red leather wing chairs by the fireplace. They smiled and murmured thanks, and Cecil was on his lanky, barefoot way to the cookshack.

Dave sat forward on the corduroy couch and looked at them eagerly. "Well? Is it a deal? Did you bring it off?"

Greenglass nodded. "Congratulations. I have all the papers with me. Sign them, and you're the new owner of Max Romano's restaurant, bricks and mortar, pots and pans."

"Marvelous," Dave said. "You're a magician, Abe." He looked at Alex. "And you'll manage it for me, Alex?"

"I can't turn down a hundred thousand a year," Alex said. "But I don't know, Mr. Brandstetter. Will anybody come? It can't ever be the same without Max."

"As long as you're cooking," Dave said, "they'll come."

Detroit City Ordinance 29-85, Section
29-2-2(b) provides: "Any person who
retains any library material or any part
thereof for more than fifty (50) cal-
endar days beyond the due date shall be
guilty of a misdemeanor."